"Jace didn't ha *idea," Asher we* ***through a conversation that he was basically winging from the very start.***

He wasn't good at this, he couldn't help thinking. He'd always been a man who was good with his hands, not with the words coming out of his mouth.

"And which idea was that?" she asked, trying to coax a conversation out of the man. He was very much the strong, silent type, she thought. That had its place, too, but right now she craved a good conversation.

"About you moving in."

He saw her eyes widen and realized his mistake.

Quick, you're scaring her off. Do something. Say something. Something smart for a change, he amended angrily.

"As his nanny, I mean," Asher blurted out.

"As his nanny," she repeated slowly.

Was he making a point of that because he was afraid she might get other ideas—or was *he* the one getting other ideas?

And if so, just what kind of ideas was he getting?

Dear Reader,

By now, you've already "ridden" through the first two Fortune books and know that the Atlanta Fortune boys, Shane, Asher, Wyatt and Sawyer, picked up and left, moved to Red Rock, Texas. The brothers bought a huge piece of property and had four sprawling homes built on it, far enough apart not to get on each other's nerves, close enough to be there for each other if the need ever arose. The reason for the boys' mass exodus was that their father handed over half the shares in the family business to a woman they had never heard of—and offered no explanation for his actions.

In Asher's specific case, he'd come out to get a fresh start for himself and his four-year-old son, Jace. Ever since the boy's mother walked out on the two of them six months earlier, Jace has been acting out. So against his better judgment, Asher accepts the help of a part-time babysitter and very quickly finds himself full-time in love with her. But Asher has a few self-doubts when it comes to his ability to make judgment calls. There are some kinks to work out on the journey to happily-ever-after. But don't doubt that they will eventually get there.

As always, I thank you for reading my books and from the bottom of my heart, I wish you someone to love who loves you back.

Best,

Marie Ferrarella

A SMALL FORTUNE

MARIE FERRARELLA

HARLEQUIN® SPECIAL EDITION®

If you purchased this book without a cover you should be aware
that this book is stolen property. It was reported as "unsold and
destroyed" to the publisher, and neither the author nor the
publisher has received any payment for this "stripped book."

Special thanks and acknowledgment to Marie Ferrarella
for her contribution to
The Fortunes of Texas: Southern Invasion continuity.

Recycling programs
for this product may
not exist in your area.

ISBN-13: 978-0-373-65728-5

A SMALL FORTUNE

HARLEQUIN®

www.Harlequin.com

Printed in U.S.A.

MARIE FERRARELLA

This *USA TODAY* bestselling and RITA® Award-winning author has written more than two hundred books for Harlequin Books and Silhouette Books, some under the name Marie Nicole. Her romances are beloved by fans worldwide. Visit her website, www.marieferrarella.com.

To
Marcia Book Adirim
for always thinking of me
when you come up with these great sagas

Prologue

"I'm sorry, Asher. I tried. I really tried, but I just can't do this anymore."

Asher Fortune looked on in complete disbelief at the woman standing at the front door. The woman with one hand on the doorknob, the other hand holding a suitcase.

The woman who, only four years ago, had promised to love him 'til death do them part.

His brain felt as if it were dashing about in a hundred different directions, desperately looking for a way to make Lynn put her suitcase down and stay.

"You need help with the house? I'll get a housekeeper for you. You need help with Jace? I can hire a nanny. Lynn, please, we can work this out," he insisted.

But when he went to take the suitcase from her, he found that he couldn't budge it. Lynn was holding on to it too tightly. Far more tightly than she was holding on to their marriage.

"No, we can't," she fired back, her voice going up almost a complete octave.

The extra volume woke their son, who had always been an incredibly light sleeper, even as a baby. Jace immediately began to cry, calling for her and adding to the cacophony of raised voices, ire and desperation that seemed to be swelling within the room.

"Don't you get it?" Lynn cried, visibly near the breaking point. "It's too late for all that. Too late for a housekeeper or a nanny." Lynn took a breath, trying to steady what was left of her disintegrating nerves. "Asher, I don't want to hurt you. You're a good man, and I don't want to hurt Jace, but this is just all wrong." She knew that now, maybe had even known it then, but he had been so persuasive, so sure they could make a go of this marriage, this family, that she had given in. "It was wrong from the start and it's my fault. I should never have told you I was pregnant. I should have just—"

"Don't say it," Asher said sharply, cutting her off. He didn't want to hear Lynn wish away their son. Wish away *his* son.

Her face was expressionless. "My not saying it doesn't make it any less true," she pointed out unhappily. "I should never have agreed to marry you, never had the baby. I'm not cut out for this."

"You haven't given it enough of a chance," Asher pleaded.

"I have given it *every* chance." Lynn's voice almost

cracked and she took a second to pull herself together. "This isn't *me,* Asher. I'm suffocating. I have to leave," she insisted, her voice quavering, sliced through with a sharp note of desperation.

Their son was still crying. Still calling. For her, damn it!

"What about Jace?" Asher wanted to know.

She sighed deeply, shaking her head. "He'll be all right." A weak smile curved her lips. "He has you."

"Listen to him." Asher gestured toward the stairs, toward their son's cries. "He's calling for *you.* He needs a mother," he insisted.

Lynn shook her head again. She tried to pull her wrist away, but he kept on holding it. "I can't be that for him. It's not who I am," she said emphatically. "Find someone else, Asher. You deserve better—and so does Jace." She looked down at the hand holding on to her wrist. "Please, let me go," she whispered.

Asher knew he could physically restrain her, but what good would that do? She was already gone.

In his heart, if he was being honest with himself, he knew that she'd left a long time ago. This person who was standing before him had only been going through the motions of being a wife and, far more importantly, the motions of being a mother. Maybe he deserved better and maybe he didn't, but one thing he was certain of. Jace, their three-and-a-half-year-old—the reason this marriage, this *sham* existed—*he* deserved better.

He deserved not to feel that the discord that existed

just beneath the surface and made itself known in a hundred different, small ways each day was his fault.

The boy, exceptionally bright for his age, already looked as if he understood in some way that his mother was upset to actually *be* a mother.

Keeping Lynn here by shaming her or bribing her would only make it worse, Asher told himself. And if Jace ever discovered the truth, it would eventually erode the little boy's self-esteem.

No, he had to think of Jace. He had to put the boy first, put the boy before his own pain because, despite everything, despite the shouting and the coldness, he still loved Lynn.

But, unlike what all those songwriters and poets maintained, love did not conquer all and love wasn't enough.

It was a sad, painful fact of life.

Without another word, Asher released his hold on his wife's wrist and dropped his hand to his side.

"Thank you," Lynn said hoarsely. "You'll be happier without me."

Lynn was gone before he could say no, he wouldn't be.

With a sigh, Asher turned away from the closed door and went to the foot of the stairs. Refusing to look over his shoulder toward the large bay window, he didn't watch Lynn walk away from the house. Away from him.

He couldn't.

He had a son who needed him.

Chapter One

"C'mon, Ash, it'll be fun," Wyatt Fortune cajoled.

He was trying to coax his older brother out of the self-imposed shell he'd crawled into ever since his marriage had blown up on him. Six months had gone by since the divorce, and even a change of venue hadn't gotten Asher to move on. It was as if Asher's soul was locked up in a dark place. His brothers worried about him.

"You've gotta meet the neighbors sometime. Why not on your own terms?" Wyatt pressed. "Besides, most of the family's dropping by, including a boatload of cousins. You know you can't hide from all of them. They'll come looking for you," Wyatt said with a grin.

Asher was doing his best to be patient, but he'd never liked being badgered, even by the brothers he loved and had followed out of Atlanta to Red Rock, at the heart of Texas.

The reason for the latter had come about as a result of an unfortunate schism with their father, the mighty James Marshall Fortune, over his secretly giving away *half* the shares to JMF to some woman nobody had ever heard of. When it was clear that their father wasn't about to disclose any of the details, he, Wyatt, Sawyer and Shane had decided to join some of their relatives who were already living in Red Rock, Texas, and they just packed up and left.

Asher had really thought that giving up his position as Vice President of JMF Financial and becoming a rancher would help him deal with things. It didn't.

The idea was that all four of them would try their hand at ranching. To that end, they'd purchased one huge piece of property where they could all live separately without tripping over one another. So four houses were commissioned and constructed on what all four of them considered to be the new family homestead. They'd dubbed it New Fortunes.

And now, after months of building, the houses were all *finally* finished.

Asher felt no different than before. He couldn't shake the feeling of being swaddled in hopelessness.

The party Wyatt was currently trying to get him to attend was being held at Wyatt's house, and it was intended to be a housewarming party for all four of them, seeing as how all their homes had been completed at the same time. Having everyone in one place made it simpler.

"You mean on your terms, don't you?" Asher asked pointedly.

"Don't get picky on me, Ash," Wyatt warned, then in the spirit of the party-to-be, relented. "All right, technically, yes, it's on my terms and at my house, but that's just because you'd never agree to having it at your place. Besides, we all know that I'm the outgoing one in the family."

"You mean the one with the biggest mouth on him," Shane, the oldest of the four, corrected, managing to keep a perfectly straight face.

Wyatt shot his brother a knowing look. They were both seen as overachievers. Neither was acquainted with the word *slacker.* "I wouldn't talk if I were you."

"That's only because I can't get in a word edgewise once you start flapping that yap of yours," Shane countered.

Asher looked on in silence. He knew what they were doing. His brothers were playing off each other for his benefit, trying to get him to come around and join in the banter, the way he used to.

But nothing was as it used to be, not since Lynn had walked out on him and on Jace, terminating their marriage.

Terminating her membership to the parenthood club, as well, by cutting off all of her ties to their son. It broke his heart to hear the boy ask for her, wondering why she wasn't coming home. Since they'd moved here, though,

Jace didn't mention her as much. Didn't ask where she was. It was as if this clean start out in the open air had muted the boy's memory.

Not so for him, Asher thought.

Still, his brothers had, in effect, thrown him a life-line when everything in his life seemed to be crumbling, both on the private front and on the work front. His ordinarily sensible, if somewhat aloof, father acting so irrationally had been almost like a final straw for Asher. It was as if the structure of his whole life had utterly collapsed.

Who just up and decides one morning to give away half the shares to an empire before breakfast? Especially without discussing it, even in passing, with the family? Granted, their father was the man at the helm, but it wasn't exactly as if the move he'd made didn't affect the rest of them. It did, grievously. Especially their poor mother.

With all this turmoil going on, his brothers were trying to unearth a bit of sunlight to shine on them. He couldn't fault them. And he certainly didn't want to be the wet blanket dampening their plans.

"Okay, sure, why not?" Asher agreed with a careless shrug. "I'll stick around for the party."

"Are you thinking what I'm thinking?" Wyatt asked, glancing toward Shane.

But it was Sawyer, the charmer of the family, who answered him. "You mean that getting big brother over here to agree was just too damn easy?"

"Exactly," Wyatt confirmed. He pinned Asher with

a look. "You're not planning a disappearing act on me at the last minute, are you?"

The thought *had* crossed his mind, but he wasn't about to say so out loud, so instead Asher replied, "Wouldn't dream of it."

"Good," Wyatt agreed with a nod. "Because you wouldn't want that precocious son of yours to be permanently traumatized by seeing his father being hog-tied and then dragged to the middle of the house warming party right in front of him, now, would you?"

"You're an evil, evil man, Wyatt Fortune," Asher declared with a shake of his head.

"That's an honorary title I promise not to take for granted," Wyatt replied solemnly, even as the corners of his mouth fought to curve. "Party starts in less than an hour. You can either hang around here until it starts or go home and get yourself back here in sixty minutes."

"You're having the party today?" Asher asked in surprise. This was fast, even for Wyatt.

"It's today." Wyatt sighed. "I already told you that two days ago. But don't worry, you have nothing on your calendar," he informed his brother. "I checked. That means you have no last-minute excuse, no being called away for a 'family emergency.' All the family that can have any so-called emergencies will be at my house tonight. As will you and my nephew." Wyatt leveled what amounted to a steely look at his older brother. "Right?"

"Right," Asher replied wearily and without any enthusiasm.

He opted to go home and change. Gone a total of forty-seven minutes, he received two calls from Wyatt, reminding him that he was due back.

The moment Asher crossed the threshold to the now noisy house, his son went flying to greet two of his uncles, Shane and Sawyer, as if he hadn't seen them in a year rather than earlier today.

Asher made his way to Wyatt instead.

Stopping before his brother, he spread his hands wide and announced, "I'm here, as promised." *Although, for how long, I don't know,* he added silently.

"Great," Wyatt declared, clapping his brother on the back as if to congratulate him for a monumental achievement. "Tell you what, why don't you pitch in and help Wendy set up?" he suggested, gesturing toward Wendy Fortune Mendoza, their cousin, who had just walked in behind Asher and his son, carrying a huge serving tray before her.

A *full* serving tray, Asher judged, if body language was any indication.

Wendy was closely followed by her husband, Marcos, who managed the local restaurant, Red, for his aunt and uncle and was responsible, in no small part, for its phenomenal success. People came to the restaurant in droves, lured by the excellent food and the heavenly desserts that Wendy created.

Red was the restaurant where Wendy had prepared the food that she and Marcos brought to Wyatt's party.

Between the two, scurrying in and out on her shaky, chubby little legs, was their daughter, MaryAnne. The toddler had a huge smile on her face and looked as if she didn't know what to get into first.

He could remember Jace at that age—except that back then, the boy had actually been tame, at least in comparison to now. At the age of just four, Jace had already managed to wear out five nannies in the six months since his mother had walked out on them. The boy went through the women as if they were so many single-ply tissues.

Nodding at a few people he recognized, Asher made his way over to his cousin, her husband and their little girl, who had just grabbed the edge of a tablecloth.

Horrified, Wendy carefully extracted the little fingers from the cloth before the union proved to be fatal for both the tablecloth and whatever dishes currently had the misfortune of being placed on it.

It was the little girl Asher focused on. "Your waitresses seem to be getting shorter and shorter these days," he commented. "Did you decide to do away with the height requirement?" he asked with a laugh, brushing a quick kiss to Wendy's cheek.

"Not quite." Wendy laughed. "MaryAnne is supposed to be off center stage," she confided. "But it seems that her babysitter is late." Still holding on to her daughter's hand to keep the child from grabbing something else, she bent over slightly so that her daughter knew she was speaking to her and said, "Look who's here, MaryAnne. Say hi to your cousin Asher."

The little girl flashed a wide smile of incredible wattage at him and then greeted him with an enthusiastic "Hi!"

"Hi," Asher echoed back. And then, straightening up again, he looked at Wendy as he nodded a greeting to Marcos. "Need any help?" he offered.

"Nope, I've got everything under control," she told him. She was gritting her teeth ever so slightly at the time as she carefully deposited the heavy tray she was carrying onto the table.

And she did, Asher observed. Wendy always had everything under control.

The realization only served to make him feel twice as bad about his own situation. Here was his cousin Wendy, formerly regarded by all branches of the family as the official family screwup, and she not only was no longer screwing up, but had settled down, gotten married, started a career for herself and had an adorable child to boot.

A child who had *both* parents coming home to her.

It was all so perfect that it made him feel as if he were living inside a disaster.

He knew he had no one to blame but himself. When he found out that Lynn was pregnant, he'd pressured her into marrying him, convincing her that everything was going to be all right.

Except that now it wasn't.

Looking back, he knew now that there could have been so many different ways to play this, to support Lynn in whatever decision she would have come to on her own. But he'd been so certain that he could somehow be all things to her, to *make* her happy.

To make her be *glad* to be a mother.

He'd been too naive at the time to know that he couldn't make a person be happy just because he wanted her to be.

He had no control over things like that.

Hell, he couldn't even find it in his soul to be happy himself. Here he was, standing on the edge of an exciting new future, with a wonderful son and a family who supported him—for the most part. He wasn't about to let his mind stray to thoughts of his father. The next move belonged to James Marshall, not to him or the brothers who had moved out here with him.

Though he tried to rein them in, his thoughts insisted on straying again and again to memories of Lynn. He'd tried his damnedest to convince her that things were going to be fine. That they were going to be perfect.

But Lynn hadn't wanted just "fine" or even perfect. She'd wanted bells and banjos and the earth moving beneath her feet, not having those feet stuck to the ground because Jace had left a huge lollipop there, just lying in wait for her.

He had to face it once and for all. Motherhood had made her feel trapped.

He had made her feel trapped.

He needed to get some air, Asher thought. Needed to clear his head before it exploded.

Asher looked around for a way to make a quiet exit and found his path blocked by Wyatt. Again. His brother was frowning, as if he was about to say something he didn't want to.

"I didn't want it to come to this, Ash, but you leave

me no choice. You've got to get on with your life, bro. Because Lynn has."

Asher looked at Wyatt sharply. "What's that supposed to mean?" he wanted to know. There was an edginess to his voice, an edginess that had completely obliterated his once oh-so-laid-back manner.

"Just what I said. She's moved on. Lynn's engaged to someone else, man," Wyatt told him, and it was obvious that having to be the one who brought the news to Asher cost him.

Asher felt as if his throat was closing up. "She's engaged?" he asked hoarsely.

"Yeah," Wyatt said quietly.

Asher felt as if someone had taken a razor blade to his heart and sliced it all to ribbons. "I guess it wasn't marriage that Lynn hated. It was marriage to *me*."

"Well, her loss," Shane said with feeling, joining them. "Remember, the best revenge is living life well," he reminded his brother, draping an arm around Asher's shoulders, as if to make sure he wasn't about to leave. "C'mon, you can be my wingman and I'll be yours," he coaxed.

"Hey, what am I, chopped liver?" Sawyer called out, overhearing.

"Nope, 'fraid you're not nearly as good-looking as pâté," Shane quipped.

"Man, we've gotta get you a pair of glasses, Shane," Sawyer fired back, shaking his head. "You're pretty much legally blind."

"Ha, you should talk. Did you actually get a good

look at that last woman you had hanging off your arm?" Shane wanted to know. "I've seen grilled-cheese sand-wiches that were sexier."

"Stop," Sawyer pleaded, his hand to his stomach. "You're making me hungry."

Asher slipped away while his brothers were shooting quips back and forth, trying to top one another.

Lynn, engaged.

Now he definitely needed to get out and clear his head, Asher thought.

This seemed like the perfect evening for it. The air was crisp, clear and surprisingly not too cold, considering that it was March.

He glanced over toward his son. Wyatt's fiancée, Sarah-Jane, was holding Jace's hand, and the boy looked smitten.

He was in good hands, Asher thought. There was no reason to worry about the boy wandering off and getting into trouble. Sarah-Jane was as responsible as they came and he knew she'd look after the boy until he got back, as would his brothers.

But first, he thought, quietly weaving his way out the back, he needed to sort things out, to get his head on straight again. He could only do that in one place—atop his horse.

He was well aware that he would have been cited by the etiquette police for just leaving the scene of a party he was technically supposed to be throwing along with his brothers, but he didn't intend to be gone all evening. Just long enough to feel less mentally stagnant.

Half an hour, tops, start to finish, he promised himself as he made his way silently out of Wyatt's newly built house.

Ten minutes later, out beneath the velvet blanket of stars, he took a deep breath of evening air.

Texas had its detractors, but he didn't number himself among them. After two months, he felt more at home here than he had back in Atlanta. He could be himself here.

Ever since he'd been a young boy, riding had always relaxed him, centered him. It had also become, of late, his favorite form of escape. He found if he rode hard, he had a fighting chance to outrace his thoughts, at least those that were weighing heavily on him.

This time was no different.

As Asher rode, not particularly looking at anything, a single thought kept drumming over and over again through his brain: How did everything that seemed so perfect go so wrong?

He hadn't a clue.

But that didn't stop him from pondering the question.

Fairly lost in thought, trying to reconstruct the bits and pieces of his life that had led to this supremely sad moment, Asher didn't even realize that he wasn't alone on the path anymore. There was a lone car, traveling at a fairly good clip, just outside his line of vision.

He wasn't even aware of the vehicle until he all but ran it off the road.

The sudden screech of tires as the driver fought to

control his vehicle abruptly chased away the detached euphoria he'd been so urgently seeking.

Reality grabbed him by the shoulders and all but shook him into consciousness. He'd almost been the cause of a horrific accident.

Turning his horse around, Asher quickly made his way back to where he'd seen the car swerve, its less than stable pattern temporarily preserved in the dirt. Concerned, his heart began to pound rapidly.

The second his horse brought him back to the dark blue sports car that had spun around several times and was now facing the wrong way, tilted unstably to one side, Asher leaped off and began to run the rest of the way.

The car had one of its rear wheels over the side of the embankment, but the other three tires were still making contact with the dirt road.

Battling a queasy feeling in the pit of his stomach at thoughts of what might have been, he crouched to be level with the door. Looking inside, there appeared to be only one person in the car.

"Are you okay in there?" he asked, peering into the dimness.

And then he saw her. The driver of the car was an absolutely gorgeous woman with long, light brown hair and brown eyes. Currently, they were flashing daggers in his direction. Somehow, that only made her look more beautiful.

And then she opened her mouth and anger came spilling out.

"What the hell is wrong with you? How could you not see me?" Marnie McCafferty demanded. "You shouldn't be on a horse, you should be walking—with a guide dog. Lucky for you I have a weakness for dumb animals."

Like a true Texan, he took offense for his horse. "My horse isn't dumb," he protested.

She fixed him with a withering look. "I wasn't talking about the horse," she snapped as she struggled to get her seat belt off and dig herself out of her seat. Swinging open her car door, she pushed him away and got out of the vehicle on her own power.

Just her luck. The tall, muscular rider with the dark brown hair was the best-looking man she'd encountered in ages, bar none, though he was clearly not the brightest bulb in the box. How else could he not have seen her?

"Where'd you learn how to ride, playing some stupid video game?" she wanted to know. The next moment, she realized she was much too close to him. He was crowding her, but she wasn't about to back up. The wind picked up and whipped her long brown hair about her face, but the woman stood her ground. "If you don't know how to handle a horse, stay out of the stable. If I hadn't swerved just then, one or both of us would be on a stretcher right now."

"I'm really sorry about that," he said, knowing he deserved the tongue-lashing. "I guess I was just preoccupied and didn't see you."

Her eyes narrowed into chocolate-brown slits. "Tell me something I don't know."

"Okay," he said gamely, "I can take you to wherever you were going." Better yet, he thought, he could take her to Wyatt's. There had to be someone back at Wyatt's housewarming who could help this woman and make sure her car was safe enough to travel.

Still angry, she looked less than taken with the offer. "Won't that interfere with wherever you were going so hell-for-leather when you ran me off the road?" she asked sarcastically.

He wasn't about to tell her that he wasn't going toward anything, but away from it. In this case, away from his thoughts.

Instead, he said, "That can wait. Besides," he went on, "I always pay my debts." He assumed, if the car didn't turn out to be in working order, that this woman would want to go to whoever her mechanic was to get her car towed and worked on. "And I'll need to know what the damages are."

Marnie shrugged carelessly, not exactly eager to have this so-called preoccupied stranger take her anywhere on the back of his horse. She didn't know the man from Adam, and she figured she was safer if she kept it that way—even if he was, on closer inspection, pretty damn good-looking.

A good-looking fool, she thought, still angry.

"Oh, you'll pay all right," she assured him. "Just give me your cell number and I'll contact you about the bill the second I know what it is."

"Sounds fair," he agreed. "But meanwhile, how are

you going to get anywhere? The car seems to be stuck and it sounded like you stripped the gears."

She knew that. That was just the problem. She also knew that her cell phone didn't get any sort of reception to speak of out here in the middle of nowhere. What that meant was that she couldn't call anyone for help.

Served her right, she thought, her anger mounting. She should never have agreed to go where the baby was, she thought now. This whole incident could have been avoided if she'd only had Wendy drop MaryAnne off at her place before she and Marcos went to cater that party they were doing tonight.

She shot another scathing look at the cowboy. Damn it, she was either stuck out here or stuck with him. "I guess I've got no choice." She was less than thrilled.

"You could always walk," he replied, getting back up on his horse.

"Very funny," she grumbled, coming up to his right side. "I was sideswiped by a vision-challenged comedian." Expectantly, she put up her hand. "Well, don't just sit there, give me a hand up," she instructed.

"Yes, ma'am," he replied, sounding deliberately contrite.

She wasn't fooled by his contrite act for a moment.

Mounting, she got as comfortable as she could, which was, at this point, not at all. She felt completely unsteady.

"You'll have less of a chance of falling off if you put your arms around me," he told her.

She didn't want to, but he was right. Reluctantly,

Marnie slipped her arms around his chest. It was, she discovered, like holding on to a rock.

"See? That wasn't so hard."

"Shut up and go," she ordered.

He kicked the horse's flanks and did just that.

Chapter Two

"Hey, wait a minute, this isn't the way to Red Rock," Marnie protested several minutes later.

Up until this point, she'd been busy trying *not* to notice things. Trying not to notice how hard this man's upper torso and abs felt beneath her arms as she held on as loosely as physically possible. And trying her best *not* to notice how unnervingly stimulating it felt holding on to him like this as his palomino rhythmically galloped along with them on his back.

But now that she *did* allow herself to notice something, she saw that rather than heading toward town the way she'd assumed he'd go, the stranger was letting his horse go in what appeared to be the opposite direction.

They were heading in the direction that *she* had originally been going before she'd been so ignobly run off the road.

"No," Marnie heard the stranger agree offhandedly, "it's not."

Everything inside her immediately tensed and went on high alert.

Was he kidnapping her?

What other explanation was there? He hadn't asked her for directions regarding her initial destination and he didn't appear to be directionally challenged. He *had* to be abducting her.

"They'll come looking for me," she warned him. "If I don't turn up, they'll come looking for me," she repeated, doing her best not to sound as if she was panicking inside.

Which she was.

"Who?" Asher asked mildly.

His deep voice felt as if it was actually *rumbling* against her hands and along her arms as she continued to hold on to him. She really didn't *want* to hold on to him, but at this point, she had no choice. It was either hold on or fall off.

"The people I was going to meet until you ran me off the road," Marnie snapped, doing her best to sound unafraid. Inside, however, she was shaking—and this time, it wasn't from anger.

"Where *were* you going?" Asher asked, half turning his head so that she could hear him more clearly. The wind had picked up and his words were in danger of being blown away if he kept his face forward.

Marnie bit her lower lip. "I was on my way to help Wendy and Marcos Mendoza out. They're catering some party for her cousins and they need help with their little girl. I told them I'd watch MaryAnne for them while they worked." Her voice grew in volume and strength as she went on. "They know a *lot* of people, and those people are going to be combing the area looking for me, so if you know what's good for you—"

He refrained from telling her that she'd just mentioned his cousins and the party they were catering was the one he'd just taken a respite from. Instead, he decided to play this out a little longer, curious as to how far she'd go with the dramatic scenario she'd just sketched.

"You smell good," he observed as the scent she was wearing wafted toward him. The wind had shifted again. The scent was something musky and sensual.

Exceedingly sensual.

The woman was sending mixed signals, he thought. That gave her something in common with Lynn. Lynn had sent out mixed signals as well—for most of their relationship together. Either that or he was just no damn good at reading women.

Probably a little bit of both, he decided, attempting to comfort himself.

"What?" Marnie cried.

More alarms went off in her head. Maybe if she jumped off the horse now and made a run for it—

To where? her brain demanded. There was nowhere to go out here, no house to run to for at least several more miles.

That was the trouble with this place, she thought darkly. The wide-open spaces were just too wide, too open, at least at a time like this.

Don't panic, she warned herself. *It's going to be all right. You'll think of something. You're not defenseless, you know....*

"Your perfume," Asher clarified, keeping his voice low. Despite her coming on like gangbusters, he had a feeling this woman spooked easily. He had absolutely no desire to frighten her. "It smells good."

"Oh," she murmured, momentarily feeling a little foolish.

Maybe he didn't mean anything by it. Maybe he actually did like the scent of her perfume. She was so accustomed to the scent she automatically put on in the morning that she not only didn't think about it but she also didn't detect it anymore. For her it just blended into the atmosphere around her, along with everything else.

All right, maybe if she dialed it down a little, sounded as calm as this stranger did, she could convince him to take her to town—or somewhere close by.

"What's it called?" he was asking her.

Her mind elsewhere, she didn't know what he was talking about. "What's what called?"

"Your perfume." Asher frowned. She sounded a little scattered to him. Maybe she had a concussion. If so, he needed to get her to a hospital. "You didn't hit your head back there, did you?"

Marnie's back was instantly up. She took his question to be criticism, not concern on his part.

"No, I didn't hit my head," she snapped at him. "I just didn't expect to be talking about perfume in the middle of nowhere with a stranger who'd run me off the road." Taking in a long breath in hopes of calming herself, she let it out again before answering his question. "It's Lavender Dreams," she told him, trying not to sound as if she was biting off the name.

Lynn had worn that, he realized. He'd bought her a bottle for her birthday. Except that it didn't smell like the same scent. But then, didn't that have something to do with mixing the perfume with a person's own scent or chemical composition, or something like that?

At any rate, the bottom line was that he found this scent to be somewhat arousing, but in a good way. What it *didn't* do was remind him of his ex.

"Just where are you taking me?" the woman suddenly demanded, although he had to admit that her voice sounded a great deal less combative this time than when she'd first challenged him.

"Home," he told her again. Well, he'd take her to Wyatt's, then head home. Promise or no promise, he was done partying for the night.

"Please," he heard her saying. "Just let me down here."

Was she really saying what he thought she was saying? "In the middle of nowhere?" he asked skeptically.

"I can walk," she told him firmly.

Was she serious? "You're not afraid of me, are you?" He had to ask. The very thought really amused him. *Nobody* was afraid of him, least of all his son, who viewed him to actually be an overgrown playmate rather than an authority figure in his life.

Yes! I'm afraid of you! her brain shouted in response to his question. However, her sense of survival had her lobbing a question back into his court by asking, "Should I be?"

"No," he told her simply.

"Then why are you taking me home?" she demanded with her very last available bit of bravado. The man was big and powerful, if that hard body was any indication. He could overwhelm her with one hand tied behind his back. And even if she made a break for it, she couldn't outrun his horse.

How did she get him to let her go?

"Well, for one thing, there's a working phone there," he told her, then decided to let her off the hook. To play this out any further would just be plain cruel. "For another, you said you were on your way to meet my cousin Wendy, and she's at the house."

"Your cousin?" she asked in stunned disbelief. "Wendy Mendoza is your *cousin?*"

"Wendy *Fortune* Mendoza," he amended. "And yes, she is."

"You're…" She paused for a second, trying to recall the name of the man whose house Wendy told her she and Marcos were bringing their food to. "Wyatt Fortune?" she asked.

"Asher," he corrected. "I'm one of the other ones. There're four of us out here. Wyatt, Sawyer, Shane and me."

In the last year or so, more than a few Fortunes had

transplanted themselves from Atlanta to Red Rock. Things had gone so well for the first invasion that a number of Fortune family members had followed, bought property and set up house, never looking back.

"You're one of the Fortunes?" Marnie asked him in complete disbelief.

He pretended not to hear the skepticism in her voice. "I am."

Oh no, it's not going to be that *easy, cowboy.* "How do I know you're not just lying to me to get my guard down?" she challenged.

His identity was simple enough to prove. "My wallet's in my back pocket," he told her. "If you reach in and take it out, you can set your mind at ease by looking at my driver's license."

Marnie balked. No way was she about to physically touch this man any more than she already had to. That was just asking for trouble.

"I'm not reaching into your pocket," she told him in no uncertain terms.

"Well, then, I guess you're just going to have to take my word for it until we get to the house."

Was she making another mistake? Marnie wondered nervously.

She felt her pulse rate accelerating again as she decided that she was going to *have* to take a look at that driver's license in his wallet.

Marnie caught her lower lip between her teeth as she inserted two fingers into his back pocket in an attempt to extract his wallet. Her first attempt failed because, using two fingers as if she were picking up a rat by its tail, her grasp was weak.

Stifling a frustrated choice word, she attempted to fish his wallet out again.

Asher turned around in his saddle again. "Want me to stop riding for a minute?" he offered.

"No!" she cried. "Just keep going."

Even though this so-called Asher Fortune might actually be taking her to his lair, she'd deal with that later. Right now she didn't want him just suddenly stopping here. He might use it as an excuse to do who knew what to her.

Okay, he had another suggestion to make. "You might get a better grip on my wallet if you used more than just two fingers."

She hated that she could almost hear him laughing at her. Rather than comment on his "advice," she braced herself and followed it.

Teeth clenched—as if that somehow helped—she yanked the wallet out of his back pocket with as minimal contact with that part of his anatomy as possible. Just as she got the wallet out, it slipped from her fingers and fell to the ground.

"Damn," she cried in frustration. They'd managed to put several yards between themselves and his wallet.

Without a word, Asher turned his horse and went back for the fallen object.

Stopping the animal, Asher began to reach for his wallet while still mounted, but he found his agility being impeded.

"You're going to have to let go of me," he told his reluctant riding companion.

Why the request brought a heated blush to her cheeks that instantly traveled up to the very roots of her hair, she had no idea. But she could definitely feel the path it took, and she was really grateful that there was next to no moonlight.

Biting back a very choice retort that was hovering on the tip of her tongue, she pulled her arms away from his upper torso as if that part of his body had suddenly caught on fire.

"Better," he told her glibly, then amended, "Or, at least, I can get the wallet this way."

His grin felt as if it had been fired directly into her chest. She couldn't remember *ever* feeling this unsettled. She had a feeling that he somehow knew it and was enjoying himself immensely.

"But on second thought, it definitely doesn't qualify as 'better,'" he told her.

She couldn't think of a single comeback to put him in his place.

And then, right before her eyes, she watched him shift in his saddle and dip all the way down from his perch to reach down on the ground. His fingers barely made contact with the wallet. Even so, he managed to scoop it up.

Like a metal tape measure rewinding itself, Asher pulled himself back into an upright position in his saddle. Marnie couldn't tear her eyes away. Though she hated to admit it, she was utterly impressed. Not many men were that flexible, she couldn't help thinking.

"Wow."

The word slipped out before she could think to stop it.

Wallet still in his hand, Asher turned and handed it to her. He figured she'd still want to verify his identity.

"Was that a compliment?" he asked, referring to the single word she'd uttered.

Rather than confirm or deny his question, she merely said, "I expected you to fall off your horse."

"Then I guess that's the sound of disappointment in your voice," he surmised.

What was he implying? That she *liked* seeing people get hurt? "I'm not a sadist," Marnie protested, annoyed at the way this man seemed to twist everything she said around.

Asher nodded at her protest. "Good to know," he answered cheerfully. They were still standing by the side of the road. He nodded at the wallet he'd just handed her. "You want to check out my identity so we can be on our way?" he suggested.

She didn't like being told what to do by someone, no matter how softly worded the order was. But since she was still holding his black leather wallet in her hand, Marnie grudgingly flipped it open and found herself looking down at his driver's license.

"It's not exactly a flattering picture," Asher conceded, "but you can see that it *is* my picture." He pointed to the name. "Asher Fortune. Feel better?" he asked.

Actually, she did, but she also felt foolish, and that didn't sit well with her. "For all I know, this is a fake. You could have picked that up at your handy, nearby forger's office."

The woman certainly did have an overactive imagination, he thought. If this was an example of what his new neighbors were like, maybe attending the party wasn't going to be half bad.

"I could have," he conceded. "But I didn't."

He said it with such simple sincerity she was tempted to believe him.

But then, she reminded herself, there were countless women lying buried in shallow graves who'd made that sort of mistake, believing the wrong man. And, given that she was all alone out here, she really couldn't afford to be too trusting.

He heard her stifle a sigh and guessed at the reason for it. "What can I do to convince you I am who I say I am?"

That was simple enough. "I'll believe you if Wendy vouches for you."

No problem there, he thought. "All right, then, we're on the same page," he said. "Since I'm bringing you to her."

Marnie chewed on her lower lip again. She still wasn't sure she should believe him, but then, he did sound pretty sincere. Maybe it wouldn't hurt to relax just a tad.

"Besides, if my intent was to 'have my way with you,'" he said, being deliberately delicate, "I would have done something by now. This isn't exactly the hub of activity out here," he pointed out, adding, "It looks like a person could be out here for days without running into anything that walked upright."

Much as she hated to admit it, the man calling himself Asher Fortune had a point, she thought grudgingly.

Marnie blew out a breath, mentally bracing herself and really hoping she wasn't going to live to regret this. *If* she lived, of course. "All right, take me to your place."

For the second time in less than half an hour, Asher kicked his heels into his horse's flanks, urging the animal on. He flashed her a grin as they galloped off. "I thought you'd never ask."

She fervently prayed that the strange, agitated feeling she was experiencing in the pit of her stomach was just due to a case of strange motion sickness arising from the fact that she was bumping along on the back of a horse—and nothing more.

Chapter Three

Fifteen minutes later, Asher brought his horse to a stop several yards from his brother's house.

A great many more guests had arrived in the time he'd been gone. From the looks of it, there were more vehicles parked around Wyatt's house than could probably be found on the lot of a standard car dealership during a regular business day.

The second he stopped, Marnie announced, "I can take it from here."

The next thing Asher knew, his reluctant travel companion was sliding off the back of his stallion. Feet back on the ground, she made straight for the front door, weaving in and out among the dormant cars like a rabbit trying to outrun an aggressive coyote.

He remained where he was for a moment, just watching her move. The phrase *poetry in motion* flashed through his head.

He supposed he couldn't blame her for trying to put some distance between them. After all, he *had* run her off the road, however unintentionally.

Rousing himself, holding on to Golden Boy's reins, he headed for the stables. Once there, he quickly removed the palomino's saddle and made sure the stallion had enough water before making his way back to Wyatt's party.

To face the music if he had to. But, with any luck, because of all these people, none of his brothers would even notice that he was gone.

The house was really crowded. He supposed that meant the party was a success. His brothers would be pleased, he thought.

"Where the hell have you been?" Shane wanted to know, suddenly appearing out of nowhere. He draped his arm across his younger brother's shoulders. As always, Shane was the picture of self-confidence. Nodding at a guest who obviously was interested in flirting with him, Shane told him, "You had the boy worried."

"Jace?" Asher questioned. That didn't sound right. When he'd gone for his less-than-successful attempt to clear his head, his son had seemed more content to be in his uncles' company than in his. Was Shane just needling him? "Why would he be worried?"

Turning so that only Asher was privy to his expression, Shane dropped his smile and said seriously, "When he realized you were gone, he thought you weren't coming back—the way his mother didn't come back."

Asher winced inwardly. "I didn't think of that," he confessed, silently upbraiding himself. In his meager defense, he'd thought that Jace was too young to make those kinds of bleak comparisons between Lynn's behavior and his own.

Now he knew better. He kept forgetting just how precocious Jace could be.

"Obviously," was Shane's for once nonjudgmental comment.

He knew that Asher was having a tough time with this divorce he'd just gone through. They all did. They might not always agree and might get under each other's skins on occasion, but at bottom they were brothers and united against the world. That world included their father, who they all felt had betrayed them without so much as a word of explanation.

"Doesn't he seem kind of young to be drawing those kinds of conclusions?" Asher asked.

"Not really," Shane answered. "Besides, he's a Fortune." The smile was back, curving the corners of his mouth. "We tend to be born old."

That was true of him, Asher thought. But not of his brothers. And definitely not Shane.

"You didn't seem to be too old to chase after that assistant district attorney back in Atlanta," he reminded Shane.

Shane dropped his arm from Asher's shoulder. He

plucked a glass of red wine from a server's tray as the man went by. "I was very young then."

Asher narrowed his eyes as he looked at him. "That was six months ago," he pointed out.

"My point exactly," Shane answered, a twinkle entering his eyes. He drained the glass and set it down on another tray. "Six months can be a very long time."

Asher shook his head. Shane tended to grow more philosophical as the evening—and the glasses of wine—wore on. "I can't even begin to pretend that I understand what you just said." Asher looked about the crowded floor, but he wasn't able to home in on Jace's whereabouts. "Where is my son?"

Arming himself with another glass of wine, Shane nodded toward the stairs and the rooms upstairs. "Wendy's nanny showed up and took charge of both Mary-Anne and Jace." His grin grew wider. "From what I saw, the kid seems pretty taken with her." Shane looked at him with that knowing look that had always irritated him. "Easy to see that he's your kid, all right. Already trying to charm an older woman."

Asher pretended to ignore his brother. It was a great deal simpler that way.

He looked around to see if he could spot either his son or the woman Shane was referring to—just in case Shane was wrong and they were still down here.

The situation Shane had alluded to went all the way back to the time just before Asher had graduated from high school. They'd had a maid back then, an extremely attractive young woman named Elena. She was two years older than he was and he'd been flattered by her attention. It was Elena who was responsible for introducing him to the world of lovemaking.

"Thanks for watching him," Asher said as he walked toward the stairs.

"No problem," Shane called after him.

There were four bedrooms upstairs. Four master suites with their own bathrooms and closets large enough to hide a small village. Jace and Marnie, as well as Wendy's daughter, were in the fourth one.

It was the only bedroom that hadn't been recruited to double as a horizontal coat closet. There were no coats littering the bed, only the two children.

"Daddy, you came back!" Jace cried the moment Asher stuck his head into the room. The little boy bounced off the bed in one swoop and ran to throw his small arms around his father's legs.

"Of course I came back," Asher said as the boy all but scrambled up his body, using him as a human jungle gym. Asher was also aware that Marnie was looking at him as if he were the spokesman for deadbeat dads everywhere. She'd probably had to calm the boy down and reassure him. Jace could be difficult to deal with once he got a notion in his head. "Why would you think I wouldn't?"

Sky-blue eyes looked up at him solemnly. "Mama didn't come back."

"Well, I always will," Asher told his son firmly. "I promise no matter where I go, I will always come back to you," he said, elaborately crossing his heart with his

free hand. "We're buddies, right?" He leaned his forehead against Jace's. It had always been part of their
bonding ritual.

"Right," the boy agreed with enthusiasm, bobbing
his head up and down. But one look at his face made it
clear that Jace had been worried.

"What that means is that we'll always have each
other's backs," Asher told his son.

"Got your back," Jace echoed.

Marnie never could hold her tongue when it came to
children—or abandoned animals. Now was no excep-
tion. "I think he'd do better with a father than a buddy,"
she told Asher.

Still holding his son in his arms, Asher shifted the
boy to his other hip as he turned to look at her. He didn't
recall asking her advice. "Oh? And what makes you
such an authority on the subject?"

In her opinion, being a part-time babysitter and children's riding instructor qualified her to speak with authority, but she refrained from saying as much. "I deal
with kids on a regular basis and see how much parents
wind up missing because they're too busy with their
lives."

He was willing to concede that he screwed up in a
number of areas, but raising Jace was not one of them.
At least he was still here to do it, unlike Lynn.

"Well, I'm *not* too busy for my son and I know what's
best for him."

"Whatever you say," Marnie said in a voice devoid
of any emotion. A voice that, *because* it was devoid of

any emotion, told him that she disagreed with him but wasn't about to waste time arguing the point.

He knew he was being overly sensitive and that she wasn't actually criticizing him so much as offering an opinion based on what he assumed she regarded as experience.

In any event, he was being too touchy. He supposed that Jace was his Achilles' heel.

"Sorry," he said. Judging by her expression, he'd managed to surprise her. He took some small satisfaction in that. "I keep getting off on the wrong foot with you."

She raised her eyes to his and suppressed an amused grin. "Two left feet?" she asked innocently.

"Sometimes it feels that way," he admitted.

Asher set his son down on the floor, and the boy immediately clambered back onto the bed to resume playing the video game Wyatt had given him earlier. Obviously curious, MaryAnne climbed back up on the bed and plopped down beside Jace.

One eye on his son, Asher turned to Marnie. "Look, let me make it up to you."

"There's no need," she demurred. While Asher Fortune was possibly the handsomest man she'd ever seen up close and personal, she had a feeling that he might turn out to be more than she'd bargained for. In general, she was used to down-to-earth working-class men. Asher was a little bit more complicated than she was accustomed to dealing with. The Fortunes were not exactly ordinary or run-of-the-mill by any stretch of the imagination.

He wasn't about to just give up that easily. He hadn't just been talking earlier when he'd told her that he always paid his debts.

"Well, let me at least pay for the repairs on your car. It's only fair."

Now that she was back among people, she'd had a chance to calm down and rethink things. It was on the tip of her tongue to turn down that offer, as well, but it wasn't as if she had money to burn. That was partially why she picked up babysitting assignments to supplement her regular income. During her days, she worked as a riding instructor at a local stable. Most of her students were children, which was just the way she wanted it. On the whole, children were a great deal easier to work with than adults.

Marnie relented. "All right, since it'll obviously make you feel better, you can pay my car repair bill," she agreed.

He wanted her to know that he wasn't just making an empty promise. "Great, I'll have someone tow your car into town. One of my brothers has this mechanic who works absolute miracles on anything that uses four wheels and a transmission."

"I don't think it needs a miracle," she said tactfully. "It just needs to be checked out." There'd been more damage done to her temper, she now silently conceded, than had probably been done to her car. She paused for a moment, debating making her own offer, then de-

cided she had nothing to lose. Besides, she rather liked
Asher's precocious son. "Look, since I'm here anyway,
why don't I take care of your son for you for the next
few hours?" She nodded toward the hallway and the
activity below. "That way, you can go enjoy yourself
at the party."

Never one for crowds, Asher suddenly realized that
he would rather have enjoyed himself here, with her and
his son. But he knew that if he said something to that
effect, it would probably sound too much like a pickup
line and he'd already made enough of a bad initial impression on her.

"I'm not much for parties," he told her honestly. "To
tell the truth, I feel out of my element with a bunch of
strangers. My brothers invited a lot of people I don't
know," he explained. He wouldn't have minded so much
if Wyatt had started with a small dinner party. But this
felt as if the whole town were here.

Her heart softened a little. Maybe that was why he'd
been so preoccupied on the road back there. He was actually trying to get away from this gathering. While she
sympathized, she had always been of the opinion that
you met challenges head-on; otherwise they conquered
you instead of the other way around.

"Well, the only way to get to know them is to get
to know them," she pointed out gently. "If you stay up
here with their coats, you'll never get to know them."

"The coats aren't the only things on this floor," he
said, looking at her for a long moment.

"I'm here, right, Daddy?" Jace piped up, pausing his game to look at his father over his shoulder.

Asher laughed and ruffled the boy's silky blond hair. "You certainly are, Jace," he acknowledged, then smiled at his cousin's little girl. "And so are MaryAnne and Miss McCafferty."

Jace scrunched up his small, open face as he pondered on the last name his father had just uttered. "Who's that?"

Marnie touched the boy's shoulder to get his attention. "Your dad's talking about me, Jace," she told him.

Jace laughed in response, as if his father had just made a really funny mistake.

"That's not Miss McCafy," he told his father, noticeably shortening his newfound friend's last name. "That's Marnie."

Asher glanced toward the woman. He'd been raised in an atmosphere that religiously clung to etiquette at the cost of approachability, as well as warmth. It was hard to shake old habits, especially the very few that actually made sense to him. Children were supposed to refer to adults by using their titles and surnames.

"You don't mind him calling you Marnie?" Asher asked her.

She looked surprised that Asher should even ask. "Why should I? It's my name."

He couldn't be that out of touch—could he? he wondered. "I was taught as a kid that it's not respectful to address adults as if they were your equal."

"Respect isn't in what name you use when you talk to

someone. It's in the way you *talk* to them, in the way you treat them," she told him just before she turned her attention to his son. "Remember that," she instructed Jace.

"Yes, ma'am," Jace answered solemnly. The next moment, he broke out in a wreath of smiles again. "Hey, Daddy, look! I'm winning!" he announced. But the moment he said that, the screen suddenly went blank. Jace's eyes grew to the size of small saucers. "What happened? Where did the game go?"

The next moment, the cause of the sudden blackout became crystal clear. MaryAnne had slipped off the bed. Trying to get back up, she tripped over the gaming machine's cord and accidentally pulled it out of the wall, bringing the game to an abrupt and ignoble end.

"She killed the game!" Jace accused indignantly, frustration echoing in his high voice.

"It's not dead, Jace," Marnie told him cheerfully, placing her body between the boy and the reason his game had suddenly gone into hibernation. If he was left unrestrained, she knew what would happen next—and she wasn't about to let it. "It's just resting."

The tears of frustration that were about to spill out halted as he stared at his new hero. "You mean like taking a nap?"

"Exactly like taking a nap," she confirmed, secretly grateful that the boy had provided her with an explanation that he was obviously willing to accept. "Machines get tired, too. Just like people do. That's why we can't overuse them."

It was obvious by the expression on Jace's small face

that he was hanging on her every word and accepting each of those words as pure gospel.

Asher stood back, taking in the scenario as it played out before him. He didn't realize he was grinning until he felt the muscles stretching. It was *definitely* better up here in this bedroom than it would be downstairs, milling around with a glass of something or other in his hand, trying to make small talk with a houseful of people he didn't know and probably, for the most part, wouldn't really *ever* know.

"You really are good with kids," he said, making no effort to hide the admiration in his voice.

"Thanks," Marnie said. "But it's not really hard. There's no magic formula. You just have to remember that they're just short people—without the baggage," she added.

Amen to that, Asher thought. He would have been a lot happier if Lynn hadn't had the amount of baggage that she'd ultimately had. Who knew? They even might still be a family now.

Who are you kidding? a voice in his head demanded irritably. *You were never a family. Lynn never wanted to be part of a family. You forced her into it and you know it.*

That part was right. He did know it. He'd talked her into having Jace, into staying and being a mother. He'd wanted it so much, wanted to have a wife and a family, to be a father, that he deliberately ignored all the warning signs flashing in front of him. Signs that told him he was heading down an incline that could only end one way: in a destructive crash.

He saw that Marnie was still looking at him expectantly.

"Really," she insisted. "This little guy'll be fine." She ruffled the boy's hair just as he had. "So, go, join the party," she urged.

"It's not my son I'm worried about," he confessed honestly, his blue eyes sweeping over her and the little girl beside her.

She laughed, getting his meaning. "We'll be fine, too," she assured him. "Now I suggest you get to that party. Wendy said that your brother Wyatt went to an awful lot of trouble to throw this little shindig. The least you can do is show up for a couple of hours."

Knowing she was right, he nodded, suppressing a resigned sigh. "You have a point," he said out loud as he turned on his heel and headed for the bedroom door.

"I always do," he heard Marnie say as he left the room.

He had no idea why that made him grin.

But it did.

Chapter Four

There was a time, Asher thought as he came to the bottom of the stairs, that he would have headed straight for the wet bar, looking to give himself several hours of respite by tossing back shots of bourbon until a velvety oblivion wrapped itself around him. Granted, that method didn't exactly solve any problems, but it did dissolve them for a few hours.

But that was before he'd become a father, before he had to think of someone besides himself and put that person's welfare before his own.

The advent of fatherhood had brought with it some heavy responsibilities, and he took his role very seriously.

Maybe, if Lynn hadn't run out on them, he might have allowed himself to relax for a few hours once in a while, given himself permission to have a few drinks rather than policing himself so stringently, silently promising to have no more than three weak drinks over the course of the evening—if even that many.

However, despite the fact that his brothers were here, Asher knew he couldn't just throw caution to the wind and be the carefree man he once was. He was an adult now and he had to act like one. That meant exercising self-discipline, as well as denial if the occasion called for it.

It was better like this, he told himself as he slowly made his way over to the open bar. This way, there wouldn't be any hangover for him to deal with and get over tomorrow morning. Plus, unlike mornings of old when the events of previous evenings were blurred and smudged, he'd actually be able to remember any conversation he might have tonight.

That was important because he felt he sorely needed a few words of wisdom to help him navigate out of this mental fog he repeatedly found himself sinking into.

His brother was right in what he'd said earlier. Asher needed to move on. But in order to do that, he needed help.

Maneuvering his way through the human obstacle course before him, Asher finally managed to reach the bar just as Marcos came up on the other side.

Perfect timing, Asher thought. Just the man he wanted to talk to.

Marcos Mendoza had been working nonstop since he, his wife and the staff he'd brought with them had arrived. He felt as if he'd been everywhere, supervising the servers and making sure that every single item they'd brought was fresh, hot and appetizing-looking. As always, he wanted to make sure that there were no complaints about either the service *or* the quality of the food that was being served.

No rest for the weary, Marcos thought when he saw his cousin-in-law come up to the bar. In an instant, he went back into catering mode.

"Asher, what can I get you?"

"I'll have a beer, thanks," Asher told him.

Moving behind the bar, Marcos paused before plucking a bottle of dark ale from amid its brethren. "You don't want anything stronger?"

The corners of Asher's mouth curved ever so slightly. "I do, but, well, Jace is upstairs and you know how it is."

No further words of explanation were necessary. Marcos understood. He'd been on his very best behavior since MaryAnne was born. For him, the decision hadn't been a hardship. He loved being a father and wanted to be able to be immersed in the experience as much as possible.

"Yes, I do," he agreed.

Popping off the top of the bottle of dark ale, he poured the contents into a tall glass, tilting it in order to keep the head of foam at a minimum. He put the glass, as well as the half-empty bottle, on the counter in front of Asher.

Studying him for a moment, Marcos asked, "How are you holding up?"

Asher took a long sip of the dark liquid, let it wind its way down, then gave a slight shrug of one shoulder. "As well as can be expected."

That didn't sound promising. Marcos decided that the well-trained staff could do without him for a few minutes and came around the bar to join Asher.

"Well, remember you've got a lot on your plate. Being a single dad's just as rough as being a single mom," Marcos told him. "I feel for you, Asher."

Asher gave him a perfunctory smile, then asked, "Mind if I ask you something?"

That was why he'd paused by Marcos in the first place. "Go ahead," he coaxed.

Asher shifted so that he could face the other man. "How do you do it?" he wanted to know. "Father, husband, successful businessman, you make it all look so effortless."

Marcos laughed and shook his head. It was far from effortless. He worked hard at all three. "Then you're obviously not looking too closely."

"Seriously," Asher prodded. "How do you make it work?"

He thought for a minute before speaking. "First off, you take it one day at a time. It takes a hell of a lot of hard work, and the truth of the matter is, I don't know where I'd be without Wendy. *She's* my rock. Wendy handles the bulk of it all," he confided. "But if you're looking for some magic formula, you're out of luck. There isn't one."

Asher shrugged, as if he'd suspected as much. "But

if there *was* a magic formula, you look like you'd be the guy who'd know about it."

Marcos knew Wendy's cousin was just being kind, but he wanted to set him straight in case he did misunderstand.

"Hey, I just got lucky and I'll be the first one to admit it. If you want to know the truth, I never thought I'd get married and I sure didn't expect that I'd *like* being married. But then," he said with a smile as he spotted his wife across the room, talking to some of her relatives, "I never expected to have someone like Wendy walk into my life, either."

Asher saw the irony in that. Funny how things turned out sometimes. "No one in the family thought she would ever settle down—or that she'd actually *stay* married if she ever stood still long enough to say 'I do' to some guy who caught her fancy."

"Well," Marcos confided, lowering his voice, "my family didn't exactly hold out any hope for me settling down, either, but I guess we surprised everyone," he said with a touch of amusement. "Wendy and I made it work—and having MaryAnne just brought the two of us closer together. Being a family is who we are." He couldn't begin to imagine his life any other way—nor did he want to.

The smile Asher offered in response was purely automatic and a little brittle around the edges. All he could think of was that having Jace was what had finally torn Lynn and him apart.

Rather than helping him to glean any lasting marital tips, talking to Marcos was only making him feel worse about his own failed marriage.

Blowing out a breath, Asher stared into the dark liquid at the bottom of his glass. "Maybe I'm just not cut out for marriage," he concluded. The thought made him less than happy.

Rather than argue the point with him, Marcos surprised him by saying, "Not everyone is." He looked up at Marcos sharply, roused from his mental funk. But before he could protest the verdict, Marcos went on to say, "My brother Miguel will probably never get married. He's much too happy being a bachelor."

"Yeah, well, maybe that's good enough for him, but I *want* to get married," Asher insisted, then added with a touch of hopelessness, "Being a husband and a father is all I've ever wanted to be."

"Then it'll happen," Marcos assured him, patting his shoulder firmly. "And if you ask me, that little boy of yours is lucky to have you. Go easy on yourself," he advised. "This kind of thing doesn't just happen overnight.

"But like I said, not everyone's cut out for that kind of life. Me, I love it," Marcos went on with feeling, "but I admit that it came as a surprise. And my brothers Rafe and Javier, they both love being married. But you say the word *marriage* around Miguel and he immediately runs for the hills. *And,*" he added, "Miguel doesn't feel as if he's missing anything." A thought hit Marcos. "Maybe Miguel's the one you should be talking to. He's happy with his lot."

Marcos straightened. It was time to get back to work.

Since Asher had asked, he left Wendy's cousin with one final thought on the subject. "Being single in a family-oriented town like Red Rock is probably harder than it would be if you lived in, say, a more urban area. You might want to think about moving to someplace like New York City."

Asher had deliberately moved out here not just to get away from his memories and the scene of what he and his brothers all felt was their father's betrayal, but for Jace, as well. He shook his head at Marcos's suggestion. "New York City's not the kind of place for me."

About to leave, Marcos paused and smiled. "You ask me, you just need a little help in settling in. The rest'll happen when you least expect it."

Given his own situation, Marcos could afford to be philosophical, Asher thought. The man was talking from the other side of a good marriage. He suspected that everything looked rosier from that point of view.

"Yeah, maybe," Asher muttered to the departing Marcos's back. But he sincerely had his doubts.

Going upstairs for his son a little later that evening, Asher tried to pay Marnie for watching the boy, but she refused to accept any money from him.

"I was here anyway," she protested softly, keeping her voice low in order not to wake the sleeping Mary-Anne who was curled up on the queen-size bed. "And having Jace around actually helped me take care of MaryAnne." She flashed a warm smile at the boy. Asher could have sworn that his droopy-eyed son puffed up his tiny chest at the praise. "They kept each other entertained. All I had to do was stay on the sidelines and make sure neither one of them got their hands on a sharp object," she threw in with a wink.

Jace responded to the wink—as did he, Asher realized. There was just something about the woman that got to him, that tightened his gut and curled his toes.

Maybe he was just lonely, Asher reasoned. All that talk with Marcos about marriage and sharing your life with someone special had made him feel lonelier than ever, even if he was truly happy for Wendy. His cousin deserved to be happy, he thought.

Don't you? a little voice in his head insisted. For once, he managed not to feel hopeless about the situation.

Thanking Marnie for her help, Asher picked up his son, who suddenly looked as if he was going to fall asleep standing up.

Finally, he thought. Jace was finally still. But Asher supposed that even a twister eventually wound down and lost momentum.

Asher carried his son down the stairs. He was definitely leaving early—from the looks of it, most of the cars were still parked outside—but he did have an excuse if any of his brothers turned up at the last moment to confront him about it.

His excuse was that, aside from taking his son home to bed, he wanted to turn in early himself. He had a long day in front of him. Mainly because he had yet to unpack all the boxes and containers that were currently littering his brand-new house.

He absolutely *hated* unpacking. But unless there was a squadron of elves looking to do a good deed, Asher knew he was going to be stuck with the job.

He supposed it would all work out in the end. If he was going to know where things were in his new house, he was going to have to be the one who ultimately put them away.

Getting an early start unpacking the next morning had been a good excuse last night when he needed to extract himself from the party, but now, confronted with boxes upon boxes of possessions, not to mention a four-year-old dynamo who had replenished his energy supply with an incredibly short nap, Asher had to admit he felt overwhelmed even before he tore the tape off the first box.

In the absence of elves, maybe he *should* hire someone to do the unpacking for him, Asher thought, looking around the family room and feeling greatly outnumbered.

Everywhere he looked, there were boxes piled on top of other boxes, creating cardboard towers.

Given the way Jace was racing around the room, weaving in and out among the tall brown towers, the boy probably saw the boxes as forming some sort of a magic village.

It was exceedingly difficult for Asher to focus with his son streaking in and out that way.

"Jace," he called out, "you have to settle down. You're going to wind up knocking something over." *Maybe several somethings,* Asher added silently, feeling his frayed nerves only becoming more so.

"No, I'm not, Daddy," Jace shouted as he continued weaving in and out. "I'm Super Jace. I can make myself real skinny so I can fit into teeny-tiny places."

Asher could feel his temper rapidly growing shorter by the second. He struggled to hold on to it. Exploding at Jace wouldn't be fair to the boy. He wasn't really mad at him; he was mad at Lynn for giving up so easy. For not wanting to fight to save their marriage. For making him fall in love with her in the first place if she'd had no intention of staying.

None of that was in any way Jace's fault.

Right now his son just wanted to play as any four-year-old did. The fact that Jace had the energy of three four-year-olds put together was just something he was going to have to get used to, Asher reminded himself. The fact that Jace *was* so energetic was why they'd gone through so many nannies back in Atlanta.

God, but he hoped the nannies in Red Rock were made of sterner stuff.

He'd just opened a box of carefully wrapped wineglasses—a wedding gift from one of his friends, he recalled with a pang—when he heard the doorbell ring.

Asher stopped for a second. He wasn't expecting anyone, and it was too early for it to be one of his brothers. They all liked to sleep in on the weekend.

So did he, once upon a time.

Asher debated ignoring the visitor and hoping he or she would go away. He started to unwrap one glass, but whoever was on the other side of the door pressed the doorbell again, more insistently this time.

The glasses were just going to have to wait, he thought with a resigned sigh.

Setting the box to one side, he called out, "I'm coming. Hold your horses." Playing a game of what appeared to be hide-and-seek with some imaginary friends, Jace ducked around another pile of boxes. "Settle down, Jace," Asher instructed for what had to be the tenth time this morning.

"Okay," Jace agreed—just as he had the other nine times.

Annoyed, struggling to remain calm, Asher yanked open the front door and bit off a terse "What?" at the person standing on the doorstep by way of an abrupt greeting.

It took him less than half a second to realize who he'd just growled at.

"Good morning to you, too," Marnie responded, her cheerful voice a direct contrast to his.

Embarrassed to be caught at being anything less than a good host, Asher immediately backtracked. The first words out of his mouth were not exactly redeeming. "What are you doing here?"

She never missed a beat as she walked in past him. "Apparently, I'm being growled at."

Chagrined, he apologized. "Sorry, it's just been kind of a really hectic morning." He hadn't gotten anything done yet, and he hated that, hated not being efficient, because that was all he had left. "But what *are* you doing here?" The second he repeated the question, what he thought was the obvious answer hit him. "Oh, God, I forgot about getting your car towed," he realized. He began to turn on his heel in order to get to the first phone within his reach. "I'll get right on it."

She caught his arm to stop him, then abruptly dropped her hand when she realized what she was doing. She was touching him, and she was better off not doing that after her involuntary horseback ride last night.

"That's okay, I took care of it already," she told him. "The car checked out all right. But that's not why I'm here," she quickly added. "Marcos and Wendy said that you need a babysitter."

Asher looked at her, confused. He had never said that to either of them. "I'm afraid there's been some mistake. Marcos talked about how he wouldn't have been able to manage on his own without Wendy, and I might have said something about envying him that. But I never said anything about needing to hire a babysitter to—"

Asher never got a chance to finish his protest because right in the middle of his sentence, there was a loud crash that sounded suspiciously like glass, followed by a bloodcurdling shriek.

An image of Jace lying on a mound of broken glass, bleeding, instantly flashed through Asher's head.

"Oh, God, Jace," was all Asher managed to say as

he whipped around and raced back to the family room, where he'd left the boy.

He should have taken Jace with him, not left him alone, he upbraided himself. Jace really *couldn't* be left alone.

Asher didn't realize that Marnie was behind him until she managed to pass him at the family room's threshold. She got to Jace ahead of him.

The box of glasses he'd just opened was upended and the entire contents had fallen out onto the tiled floor. Every single glass appeared to be a casualty of the collision.

Jace was just picking himself up off the floor, dazed but apparently unhurt. The shriek had been a result of surprise, not pain.

"I'm sorry, Daddy," Jace said, apologizing. "Super Jace crashed."

Asher's knees suddenly felt weak when he thought of what could have happened but didn't. Rather than yell at the boy, or say something about having just warned him not to run in the room, Asher sank down to the boy's level and hugged him.

"Are you all right?" he wanted to know.

"Uh-huh." Jace vigorously nodded. "But the glasses got hurt."

"I can get new glasses," Asher told him. "I can't get a new you."

Marnie was standing just off to the side, observing the interaction between father and son, and she felt her heart quicken in response to what she'd just heard

Asher tell Jace. It didn't occur to her then, but much later, when she reflected back to this scene, she realized that this was the moment she began to fall in love with Asher Fortune.

Chapter Five

"Do you want me to sweep or to occupy?" Marnie asked him after he'd released the boy from his embrace.

Rising to his feet, Asher looked at her, unable to make any sense out of her question. "Excuse me?"

"Do you want me to sweep up?" She gestured to the scattered shards of broken glass that seemed to be absolutely everywhere. "Or to occupy your son while *you* sweep?" She nodded at the little boy standing beside him. "I figure one of us can do one task while the other can do…the other," Marnie finally concluded, unable to find a better way to word her offer.

He definitely didn't want Marnie doing anything that even vaguely smacked of housekeeping, but the latter part of her suggestion would really be helpful. Whenever Jace helped him with anything, it usually took him at least twice as long to get the thing done.

"If you don't mind keeping Jace busy, I'd really appreciate it. Otherwise, I know I'll have another set of more-than-willing hands trying to help me pick up all the broken slivers of glass, and I've got this really uneasy feeling that we could very well cap off our day with a trip to the emergency room."

Her thoughts exactly.

About to guide the little boy gently but firmly into another room, Marnie took a good look around. Everything appeared to be a chaotic, jumbled-up mess. The boxes made it hard to get around. The broken glass didn't exactly help. It looked to be too much for one man to deal with.

"Sure you don't want me handling cleanup?" she asked Asher one final time.

He really did hate unpacking, but it was something he was going to have to face. There was no getting away from that.

Reluctantly, he turned her down. "Not that I don't appreciate the offer, but keeping Jace away from the scene of his crime is more than enough, thanks."

Marnie nodded. "Okay, whatever you say," she agreed. "I'm here to help."

"About that," Asher began as he started to pick up and deposit the largest shards of glass into the box that had held the glasses when they had been in their previous, far more solid state.

She looked at him expectantly, waiting. "Yes?"

He wanted her to know that this wasn't his idea. He didn't want to come off as some whining individual, complaining about not having anyone to palm his son off on.

"I really didn't say anything to Marcos about needing a babysitter."

"I believe you," she said simply. "From my experience, Marcos is a pretty intuitive guy. Maybe he just read between the lines and assumed that since you were a single dad, you needed someone to take care of your son while you were working—or do you already have someone lined up for that?" she asked as the thought occurred to her. Maybe that was why he hadn't actually said anything to Marcos about needing a babysitter or a nanny. He'd already taken care of that.

"No, but I'm still working that out," Asher said vaguely.

It wasn't a lie; it just wasn't exactly the truth. The current situation *was* something that was in flux at the moment.

He'd been putting off interviewing babysitters and nannies because of his previous less-than-successful experiences. Between his divorce and the caregivers who had not walked but run from his employ, not to mention his son, he felt that he no longer had the ability to make a good judgment call as far as the fairer sex went.

"All right." What he was telling her, she thought, was that although he did need someone to watch his son, he wasn't about to make a commitment to anyone just yet. *Fair enough,* she thought. "Why don't we just take it one step at a time here?" Marnie suggested tactfully.

He couldn't very well argue with something that sounded so reasonable.

"Okay," he agreed tentatively. "So, is this what you do for a living?" he wanted to know. "Babysit? Or I guess the proper term for that is being a nanny." There was a difference. For one thing, nannies were paid more and all but lived with the child.

If she actually *was* a nanny and he hired her, that would mean she'd be moving in....

Asher realized that he was allowing his mind to drift into uncharted waters, and he quickly reeled it in.

"In a manner of speaking, but not full-time," she began to explain.

He guessed at what she was about to say. "Business bad?"

"No." On the contrary, she'd actually had to turn down several offers. She'd come here not because of anything Marcos had said to her but because there was something about Asher that had told her he needed help. She was a complete sucker when it came to things like that. "That's what I do on the side mostly. I actually started babysitting as a favor for friends...." She paused, grinning. "I guess in a way I'm still doing that."

"If you just do it on the side, what do you do the rest of the time?" he asked, curious. The next second, he realized how intrusive that had to sound. He backed off instantly, raising his hands as if in surrender. "Sorry, none of my business."

She laughed. She'd been subjected to far worse than what he'd just asked. "That's okay. It's not like I'm a spy or anything like that."

Jace's eyes grew huge. With a child's brand of selective hearing, he only heard what he wanted to. And he had heard that.

"A spy?" he echoed in what had to be the loudest whisper she'd heard in a long time. "You're a real spy?"

"No, sweetie, I'm a real riding instructor. I teach kids how to ride. I love horses—and kids," she explained, ruffling his hair, "so teaching kids how to ride just seemed like the natural thing for me to do."

"Me, too!" Jace declared.

"You, too?" There wasn't so much as the hint of a smile on her lips as Marnie asked the boy, "You teach kids how to ride?"

"No, silly." Jace giggled, waving his hand at her. "I love horses, too."

"Oh, well," she said slowly, mulling over the next words she was about to say, "maybe your dad can bring you by someday and I'll give you a lesson—on the house," she added in case Asher thought she was just trying to make more money.

"I don't want to ride a house," Jace protested, "I want to ride a horse."

"That, too," she said, this time not bothering to suppress her smile.

Asher caught himself staring at it, and at her. It was an exceedingly captivating smile, he thought. The kind of smile that didn't just register with a person in passing, but registered with that person's soul. In this case, that would be him. He found that it was an infectious smile, that caused whoever saw it to smile, as well.

Widely.

Marnie deliberately broke eye contact first. She was starting to feel something unsettling taking hold and there was no time for something like that. Her schedule was much too full.

Turning her attention to the small boy standing between them, she said, "Jace, how would you like to show me around your new house?" She saw the boy light up like the proverbial Christmas tree. "I'd love to see it."

"Sure!" Jace agreed with the kind of enthusiasm befitting a child who had never been intimidated by anything. Taking her hand in his small one, Jace quickly tightened his fingers around it—in case she changed her mind about the tour. "Wanna see my room first?" he asked her.

"I would *love* to see your room first," she told him, mimicking his enthusiastic tone.

Jace's eyes all but sparkled as he tugged on her hand, ready to pull her out of the room if need be. "Then c'mon!"

She glanced over her shoulder at Asher just before she and Jace disappeared around the corner. "We'll be gone for a while," she promised.

"Sure, take your time," he urged. He could use all the time she gave him. Getting all the shards picked up, he judged, was going to take more than just a few minutes.

* * *

He'd cleaned up the mess that Jace had accidentally created and had even managed to unpack, as well as put away, the contents of four boxes before Jace and the guest he continued to have a firm grip on returned to the family room.

Keenly aware of the amount of time that had passed— a good ninety minutes—Asher looked up at them as his son, the tour guide, and Marnie walked toward him.

"About time you got back," he said to Jace, deliberately keeping a straight face as he pretended to be stern with the boy. "I was just about to send out a search party."

Jace's light eyebrows furrowed together over his forehead. "What would they be searching for, Daddy?"

Asher laughed. "You, of course."

"But I knew where I was," Jace protested, confused why his father would need help finding him. "I was right here. With Marnie. I mean Miss—" Jace stumbled verbally as he tried to recall the name his father wanted him to use when he was talking about the lady with the nice smile.

"That's okay, Jace," Marnie interrupted, aware of what the little boy was attempting to do. "You can call me Marnie, remember? I said it was okay with me— and your dad," she deliberately added since that was the part that was supposed to carry weight with the boy.

"Oh, yeah," he recalled. Never one to blatantly be disrespectful, Jace turned around to look at his father to confirm the permission he'd just been reminded about. "Is it still okay, Daddy?" he asked politely.

Asher was just too tired to offer any arguments to the contrary even if he wanted to. "It is with me if it is with Miss McCafferty," he told his son.

Like two tiny tennis balls being lobbed over the net at the exact same time, Jace shifted his eyes to look at Marnie, silently asking if it was still okay with her since his dad had left the decision up to her. He had just made up his mind that he wanted Marnie to be his new mom, and he didn't want to do or say anything that would make her go away.

"Absolutely," she responded. "Besides, McCafferty is a pretty big mouthful to say, isn't it?" Jace bobbed his head up and down. She got the feeling that he would agree with anything she had to say. "I wouldn't want you choking on that," she told him solemnly.

Jace took her words as gospel, the way he seemed to take everything that came out of Marnie's mouth, Asher noticed. The next moment he realized that he could very well be looking at the woman who had inspired his son's very first case of puppy love.

The boy, he caught himself thinking, had very good taste.

The next moment, Asher brushed the thought quickly away.

Marnie glanced at her watch. She still had some time left before she was due at Coventry Stables to teach her afternoon students.

"You men hungry?" she asked.

"Yes!" Jace instantly answered.

"He's always hungry," Asher told her, looking at his son with an affectionate smile.

"That's understandable," Marnie said. "He's a growing boy. He needs fuel to grow."

Jace looked at her uncertainly. "I don't eat fuel," he protested. "I eat food."

"I know, but food turns into fuel in your body," she explained.

He was having difficulty processing the information. "Like in a car?" he asked, amazed.

Marnie smiled at him, humor crinkling her eyes. The boy was nothing short of adorable.

"In a way," she agreed. "Anyway, we're getting off the subject. It's almost lunchtime. I thought I'd make you two something to eat before I left."

Jace's face fell. He had obviously not thought about her having anywhere to go. "You're leaving?"

"Uh-huh. After I make you something to eat," she repeated. "I've got students to teach. Can't have them just sitting around on their horses, not going anywhere, can we?"

Jace shook his head. "No," he said because he could tell that was the answer Marnie wanted him to give.

Knowing that the best way to get the boy to smile again was to make him feel useful, she asked, "You want to help me make lunch?"

She was right. Jace broke out in a huge smile as he loudly declared, "Yes!" and immediately put his hand in hers.

"You won't find much in the refrigerator," Asher warned, calling after her.

Sarah-Jane, Wyatt's fiancée, had been nice enough to put a few things into his refrigerator to tide them over, but that had been a few days ago and there wasn't much left. He hadn't gotten a chance to get to the grocery store yet.

"That's okay, I know how to make do," she assured him.

And she did.

Returning twenty minutes later—enough time for him to unpack yet another box completely and begin unpacking a sixth—Marnie came in carrying two plates, one in each hand.

What looked to be two tostada shells—one per plate—had been filled to the brim with a potpourri of ingredients she had located both in the refrigerator and the pantry.

When Asher looked more closely, he saw that there were bits of shredded romaine lettuce, diced tomatoes, some finely shredded cheese—cheddar, from the color—black beans, green onions, from the smell of them, and it looked as if she'd put the last piece of leftover roast chicken to use by dicing it up and sprinkling that, too, inside the crisp shell. It was all topped off with the last of the salsa she'd apparently located.

Asher hadn't realized he'd had half the things she'd come up with. Marnie was good, he couldn't help thinking.

The moment he got to see the results of her efforts, he realized just how hungry he really was.

His stomach actually growled. He hadn't bothered to eat breakfast this morning, putting off making something for himself for one reason and then another until he just completely forgot about the meal altogether.

Until now.

What Marnie had come up with looked a good deal better than anything he could have thrown together for breakfast, Asher thought. He wasn't much for cooking.

"I had all that in the kitchen?" he asked incredulously.

"Just took a little looking," she answered, "but yes, you did. I cleaned almost everything out, though," she admitted. "So you're going to have to go to the supermarket to replenish everything. Soon," she emphasized when he didn't say anything in response.

Asher wasn't aware that he was frowning—grocery shopping did not number among his favorite pursuits—but Marnie noticed immediately as she turned the coffee table into a makeshift dining area for Asher and his son.

"I could take care of that for you if you like," she offered. "Go grocery shopping," she clarified in case he wasn't following her. "As long as you give me a list of what you want me to buy."

He stopped eating and looked at her in complete surprise. "You'd do that?"

He made it sound like such a big deal, she thought, when it really wasn't. She raised and lowered her shoulders in a casual shrug. "Sure. I can do it at the same time I do mine. No big deal."

Asher couldn't help asking the next question that rose to his lips. Having been burned by a person he trusted so much, he had become naturally suspicious of seemingly selfless offers of help. He just wasn't accustomed to Good Samaritans.

"Why?"

The question made her somewhat uncomfortable. Not because by asking that, he appeared not to trust her, but because the question made her remember her mother's take on her good deeds. Her mother tended to think she went overboard when she tried to help.

"Why not?" Marnie countered. There was a smile on her lips, but she had raised her chin slightly. "It's called being neighborly."

What she didn't add was something else that her mother had criticized her for. Something that was, ultimately, a fact of life in her case. There was no point in denying it. She had a weakness for strays and seemingly lost creatures, be they the human variety or the four-footed kind. She'd find her heart going out to them and she just couldn't get herself to turn her back on the lost, needy look in their eyes.

The same kind of look, she thought, that she saw in Asher's eyes.

"Can I go shopping with you when you go?" Jace asked excitedly, all but bouncing up and down on the sofa, his feet waving back and forth beneath the coffee table as he looked adoringly up at her.

She knew that if the occasion did arise and Asher did ask her to do his grocery shopping, she would make far better time on her own without Jace. But she wasn't about to disappoint the energetic little boy for the world. No matter what sort of reasoning she used or how gentle the explanation, all Jace would come away with would be the word *no,* which was why she told him, "I'm counting on it."

Jace's grin nearly split his face in two.

Chapter Six

Watching his son interact with the woman whom Marcos had misguidedly sent his way, Asher couldn't help marveling at the absolute joy he saw radiating on Jace's face. He hadn't seen the boy this happy since—

He realized that he couldn't actually remember a time when Jace had been *this* happy. Not since before Lynn had removed herself from the boy's life.

Certainly the boy hadn't reacted this way to any of the nannies Asher had brought into their home back in Atlanta after Lynn's abrupt departure.

Despite the fact that all five of those women had been markedly different from one another, varying in age, experience and approach—some had been strict, some had been so lax they appeared to be almost disinterested—the one thing they'd all had in common was several weeks into the job, they had all handed in their resignation and then run for cover, going, he imagined, as far away from Jace as they could.

Jace, they had all stated in one way or another, was just too much for them to handle.

Asher supposed that it wasn't really right to form a lasting opinion after only two hours into the relationship between his son and Marnie, but he had to admit that Jace's positive reaction certainly helped tip the scales heavily in Marnie's favor.

So much so that when she got up to leave, he found himself feeling almost as disappointed as he sensed that Jace was. The fact that he did feel that way took Asher by surprise. He told himself he was only empathizing with his son, nothing more.

"Do you hafta go?" the boy asked as he followed his new best friend to the front door.

She turned from the door to face the boy. "I'm afraid so. I've got those students waiting for me, remember?"

Jace's lower lip stuck out in a sorrowful pout. "Can't they wait a little longer?"

Marnie smiled at him, touched by his obvious instant attachment. But she knew that she was walking along a very narrow ledge. She had to be careful not to encourage him to become even more attached to her. The goal was always to make any child she dealt with as independent as possible for his own good.

Cupping Jace's chin in her hand, she smiled down at the small, puckered face as the boy's eyes held hers. "You always have to remember to honor your commitments, Jace," Marnie told him. "That means always keeping your word when you give it."

Jace sighed and nodded. "Okay. You gotta go," he murmured, resigned.

Since she was actually leaving, Asher wanted to settle up. He took his wallet out of his back pocket and extracted several large bills. He held them out to her. "How much do I owe you for today?" he wanted to know.

Marnie gently pushed aside his hand. "Nothing," she assured him.

Asher frowned. He thought of last night. She hadn't accepted any money from him then, either.

"You realize that you're never going to get ahead if you keep giving away your services for free," he told her, then tried again. "Now, what do I owe you?"

"Nothing," she repeated, still smiling at him. "Really," she insisted. "Marcos already took care of it for you. He said it was his treat."

He didn't like being in debt to anyone, even if it was someone he liked, like Marcos. Asher made a mental note to have a talk with his cousin's husband the first chance he got. Granted, Marcos was a successful businessman, but Asher wasn't exactly a charity case here.

"You'll come back?" Jace was asking Marnie as she opened the front door.

Rather than just make an empty promise to placate the boy, Marnie looked over Jace's head at his father. "That depends on your dad," she told him.

"He wants you back," Jace told her, then glanced at

his father, waiting for him to agree. When he didn't, Jace prodded, "Don't you, Daddy?"

Rather than use the word *want* in reference to the woman, something that felt much too personal, much too intimate—a result of the blow Lynn had dealt both his ego and his self-esteem—Asher said, "Jace certainly has taken a shine to you."

"The feeling," she replied, smiling down into Jace's upturned face again, "is definitely mutual." She raised her eyes to Asher's. She could see a hint of discomfort there and wondered what that was all about. The man had baggage, and she didn't want to add to it. "See you around, Mr. Fortune," she said just before she closed the door behind her.

"We'll see her around, right, Daddy?" Jace asked, seeking assurance. "Right?" he repeated when his father didn't say anything to him.

"Sure," Asher answered mechanically, knowing that if he didn't, Jace would keep after him until he got the answer he wanted.

Jace made a beeline for the sofa that was butted up against the large bay window. The window looked out onto the driveway. Scrambling up on the cushion, he stood waving madly as he watched the lady who had come to his house walk to her car.

"She's looking, Daddy, she's looking!" Jace cried excitedly. "Wave!" he pleaded. When his father didn't join him at the window, the boy remained where he was, waving frantically with both hands. "C'mon, Daddy. She won't come back if you don't wave."

There were times, Asher thought as he crossed over to join his son, when Jace took his breath away, displaying glimmers of rare insight that were far beyond his young years.

It came as no surprise to Asher that the very next day, Jace asked after the young woman he'd taken such a shine to. Asher would have been far more surprised if his son *hadn't* asked him if she was coming that day. But the boy's query, repeated several times over the course of the morning, still didn't make him drop everything and put in a call to her.

"Why don't we see how we manage for ourselves first?" he finally suggested.

It wasn't that he had found fault with the woman Marcos had sent his way. From where he'd been standing, she seemed pretty much flawless.

Almost unnervingly so.

And it certainly wasn't because he didn't like her. He did. Maybe more than he was comfortable with, but that wasn't why he wasn't putting in a call to her for her services, either. Asher simply felt that it pointed to a lack of character on his part if he actually admitted that he needed help.

But by the third day, as he continued taking his life out of the various cardboard boxes while Jace seemed determined to become a whirling dervish, Asher was willing to admit that maybe his ability to stay on top of everything while also taking care of Jace was woefully overrated.

With equal feelings of dread and anticipation, he took the card that Marnie had left behind—the one with her cell phone number on it but not her landline, he noted—and began to tap the numbers out on his cell.

He heard the phone on the other end of the line ring four times. On the fifth go-round, he heard a clicking noise and knew his call was being transferred to voice mail.

A product of the electronic age, he still hated having to talk to some inanimate machine. He'd call back, he decided.

Asher was about to terminate the connection when he heard a noise on the line. Quickly bringing it back up to his ear, he said, "Hello?"

"Hello?" the voice on the other end echoed. It was Marnie. It unnerved him slightly when he realized that he knew her voice instantly. It was obvious, though, that she didn't recognize his voice, but then, why should she?

But rather than his identifying himself, the next word he uttered was "Help."

"Mr. Fortune." It wasn't a question but a statement. A statement with a touch of amusement in it.

He'd never really liked being addressed by his surname. For a very specific reason. "Mr. Fortune is my father," he told the woman in a crisp, emotionless voice. "This is Asher."

He could almost hear Marnie smile as she replied, "Yes, I know. I was beginning to think that you'd decided to go with someone else."

She'd said as much to Wendy when the latter called

to find out how she liked working for Asher. Wendy had told her that wasn't possible since Asher really didn't know anyone else to hire.

"I could have just lost your number," Asher pointed out.

As far as she was concerned, that hadn't even been a consideration. "You don't strike me as the type to lose anything," she told him simply. Besides, if he had lost her number, he could always have called Wendy or Marcos for it.

Asher laughed as he looked around the absolute chaotic mess that surrounded him. All his rooms looked like this one to varying degrees.

When had he accumulated all this stuff? he couldn't help wondering.

Unable to deal with his emotionally crushing situation at the time, he'd opted to allow the movers to pack everything up for him. Seeing the result now, he realized what a colossal mistake that had been on his part. Although the moving company had come highly recommended, the actual movers involved obviously had no regard for rhyme or reason when it came to packing. And although the boxes had been labeled "master bedroom" and "den," the contents of all the boxes he'd opened so far had items in them that had no place in the rooms they were purported to belong in.

Between that and his son's maddeningly frequent bursts of pure, unadulterated frantic energy, Asher felt overwhelmed, outnumbered and just plain exhausted beyond words.

"You obviously haven't seen me unpack," he said now to Marnie.

"Yes, I have," Marnie pointedly reminded him. "The other day, when Marcos sent me over, remember? You were hip-deep in boxes at the time."

"Well, it's gotten a whole lot worse since then," he told her, the weariness he felt seeping into his voice despite his best efforts to keep a lid on it, at least until the woman got here. "Can you come over?"

He hadn't specified a date yet, or a time. "When?" she asked.

"Yesterday," he said honestly. "But I'll settle for whenever you can get here today."

For a second, she thought he was just being funny, but then she realized that he was serious.

"To help you unpack?" she asked since he hadn't mentioned Jace. He made it sound as if it was the unpacking that was getting to him, not his free-range son.

"To tire out Jace if you can," he said in a moment of weakness. "Barring that, if you could just keep him busy in any room that I'm not in, that would be a tremendous help right now."

So it *was* to babysit, she thought. Marcos and Wendy had been right. Jace's dad was a stubborn man who didn't like asking for help because he felt he had something to prove.

"I take it that Jace is being too helpful?" Marnie guessed.

She heard Asher sigh wearily on the other end before answering her. The sound seemed to come from the bottom of his toes and was, whether or not he realized it, an answer in itself.

"You don't know the half of it," he said.

Rather than ask why he hadn't called her sooner, Marnie felt sorry for him. She could feel her sympathy kicking into high gear. "Well, my last student just called to cancel because she has to study for a make-up exam, so I can probably be at your house within the hour."

Asher felt instantly better. He refrained from saying that he would be counting the minutes.

Instead, he just told her, "Great! Jace will be really happy to see you." *And I will, too,* he added silently.

Saying so out loud, though, would be admitting too much and it might, he told himself, give her the wrong idea. He definitely didn't want to scare her off since, to date, she was the best babysitter he had managed to find.

Asher began to whistle the moment he ended the call. The cavalry was coming.

His doorbell rang exactly twenty-three minutes later.

On his knees beside a box he'd just emptied, Asher looked up sharply.

Marnie.

Uttering a quick prayer of thanksgiving, Asher dusted off his hands and got up off his knees. He kicked the box he'd just gutted out of the way and quickly made his way to the foyer.

The door was already open by the time he reached it.

Asher's considerable relief at seeing Marnie standing

in his doorway was somewhat diluted by the fact that Jace had gotten there ahead of him. Since the door had been locked, that meant that his son had been the one to open it. This despite Asher's countless lectures to the boy about never opening the door to *anyone*.

"What did I tell you about opening the door, Jace?" Asher asked him sternly the moment he reached him.

Overjoyed to find Marnie standing on the threshold, Jace now looked at his father in obvious confusion. It was apparent that the boy didn't understand what he had done wrong.

"You said not to unless you were there."

If he knew that, then why had he opened the door? "Well?"

"But you were there, Daddy," Jace pointed out. "You were in the house. I heard you yelling at the boxes when the doorbell rang."

Embarrassed and not wanting to come off like some kind of fool who talked to inanimate objects, Asher protested, "I wasn't yelling, I was…"

"Discussing things," Marnie injected helpfully when she saw that Asher was struggling to find the right words to defend himself. No hint of a smile graced her face, although it did manage to come out a little in her voice.

"Besides," the boy went on, "I had to let her in. I didn't want her to go away."

So saying, the boy took a firm hold of her hand and tugged on it, wanting Marnie to come into the house, afraid that she might change her mind and leave.

For such a small boy, he really did have a very strong grip, she noted, as she allowed him to draw her into the foyer.

Jace continued hanging on to her hand.

"I would have waited," she assured the boy. "If I had to, I would have rung the doorbell again. Several times." She looked into the boy's eyes. "Your dad's right, you know," she told him quietly. "You shouldn't open the door when he's not standing right there next to you. Promise me you won't open the door again unless he or some adult you know is with you?"

She didn't want to say anything either more graphic or stern because she didn't want to rob Jace of his innocence or his confidence that he was safe in his own home. She didn't believe in frightening a four-year-old. She didn't want him being afraid, just careful.

There was a very fine line between the two, and it wasn't the easiest one to navigate, but it was well worth the trouble. Jace had a right to be a happy child for as long as possible.

"Okay," he told her cheerfully, "I promise." He was still holding on to her hand. "Are you gonna stay?"

She looked at Asher. "Yes, I am. For a while," she qualified.

That was all he wanted to hear. At four, Jace was still living in the moment.

"Cool!" he declared with even more than his usual enthusiasm. "I got a new video game. But I kinda don't know how to play it," he confessed.

It was a game that Wyatt's fiancée had given to the boy.

"I haven't had a chance to read the directions to explain it to him," Asher confessed.

"That's fine, I can do it," she volunteered. Turning to the boy, she told him, "Looks like you're in luck, Jace. I just happen to be very fluent in video-game-speak."

The upturned face was full of wonder as well as adoration. "Is that good?"

"Yes. That's very good. All right, take me to your game," she instructed Jace playfully.

"You bet!"

This time, the sigh she heard escaping Asher's lips just as she left the foyer was one composed of sincere relief.

Hearing it made her smile.

Chapter Seven

Over the next several weeks, Marnie felt like she was getting to be a fixture around Asher's house.

Whenever she wasn't working at the stables, teaching a small, eager group of preteens and teenagers how not just to ride well, but also to respond to the different signals their horse was giving them, she was at Asher's place. Initially, it was just to occasionally watch his son and all that entailed.

But what she did, while always including Jace, began to spread out. She took the boy to the grocery store to restock Asher's refrigerator and pantry. And, to pass the time and because he asked her about it, she started giving Jace horseback-riding lessons. Granted, the pony was of the large, plastic variety that only moved up and down, but it was a start.

While Marnie still referred to what she was doing as babysitting, it seemed to her as if what had begun as a part-time job was taking on all the ramifications of a full-time nanny position.

Although she had no way of knowing, it felt the same way to Asher.

Each time he said goodbye to Marnie, he was fairly certain that he wouldn't be seeing her for a while, that, because Jace was such an angel around her, things were finally beginning to work themselves out for the better. In this case, it meant that things were going back to the way they'd been in the household before his marriage had split in half.

Unfortunately, it didn't quite work out that way when Marnie wasn't around. Right before his eyes, it was as if his son had turned into two entirely different little boys.

When he and Jace were alone, while not being out-and-out disrespectful, the boy definitely became far more than just a handful to deal with. Though Asher hated to admit it, Jace had become a maddening challenge to him at every turn.

So much so that Asher was finding himself surrendering sooner and sooner, mentally waving a white flag as he reached for the phone in order to call Marnie for help.

Mercifully, she'd always agree to come over. And every time, the second she walked across the threshold, Jace would suddenly transform. The whirling dervish would disappear and the little angel would take his place.

He was still full of energy, but that energy was easily harnessed and redirected. The boy was nothing if not on his very best behavior around Marnie.

If this change occurred once or twice, Asher might not have thought anything of it. But since it happened every single time, it was the cause of some concern for him. Why couldn't he control his own son? He certainly loved the boy enough. What was he doing wrong?

He would have put the question to Marnie if Jace hadn't left him so utterly worn out by the time he called her for help.

"Hi!" Jace all but crowed happily the second the front door was opened and Marnie walked in, having come straight from the stable.

True to his word, the boy hadn't opened the door on his own even though he knew it was Marnie and he was eager to see her. But he was right there, closer than a shadow beside his father, when the latter unlocked the door.

"I put all my toys away like you wanted me to," he dutifully informed Marnie.

It was the last thing she'd said to him when she'd left last night. She'd told him that he needed to put his toys away neatly after he finished playing with them each day.

"Very good," she said, smiling her approval. "I like a man of his word." Out of the corner of her eye, she saw the completely stunned expression on Asher's face. "What's the matter?"

Asher looked incredulously at his son. "His room

was a total disaster area half an hour ago. It looked like two toy stores had exploded. I told him to clean up his room and he just said, 'Later.'"

"Well," Marnie said, pretending to mull over what he'd just told her for Jace's benefit, "technically, this *is* later. So, as long as he did clean up, that's what really matters." Turning toward Jace, she put her hand out to the boy. "Let's go up to your room and see how well you did," she suggested.

"Sure!" Jace agreed eagerly. He liked the way she smiled when he pleased her.

"This I've got to see," he said.

When Asher walked into his son's room, it didn't look like the same place he'd seen earlier that day. The bedroom was nothing short of spotless, so neat, in fact, that it looked like something that might have been photographed for a magazine.

Looking at it, Asher found himself temporarily speechless. It was, he thought, as if he'd suddenly slipped into some parallel universe.

"It sure didn't look like this half an hour ago," he murmured, more to himself than to Marnie.

She, in turn, smiled down at Jace. "See what you can do if you try?" she asked him.

The boy beamed in response to what he took to be a seal of approval from the woman who had won his young heart.

She glanced at Asher over her shoulder. "You called me half an hour ago," she reminded him.

He knew that. The room had been the final straw that

had caused him to call her this time. Asher looked at her now, not sure what her point was. "Yes, so?"

Lowering her voice, she gave him a suggestion. "Carry that to its logical conclusion." She didn't want to come out and say it, especially not in front of the boy, but it was obvious that Jace was behaving this way for a reason. Then, turning toward Jace, she said, "Didn't you say you had a new book you wanted to show me?"

Because he was pleased that she remembered what he'd told her just before his dad had ended his call to her today, Jace's face lit up even more brightly, if possible. "Yeah, you wanna see it?"

"I've been thinking about nothing else," she told him with a very straight face.

"Really?" Jace asked. If he appeared to be any more pleased, he would have been walking several inches off the floor.

"Really," she told him solemnly.

Okay, so it wasn't really strictly true, but she wasn't ready to admit what actually *had* been preying on her mind to a far greater extent.

Besides, she didn't think it would be exactly appropriate for her to tell the little boy that his father had all but become a fixture in her brain. A fixture that she could pretty much keep at bay during her waking hours.

But when she was asleep, all bets were definitely off.

It felt as if Asher Fortune was beginning to all but haunt her dreams.

Asleep, she had no defenses against the very real, growing attraction she felt for him. An attraction that only seemed to become stronger and stronger every time she was around the man.

But at least she was awake then.

Awake, when she was with him, she had her banter, her wit, her humor to help serve as her shield. She was fairly confident that Asher didn't have a clue about her feelings for him, or the fact that every time she heard his voice on the other end of her cell, even before he got to the part where he asked her if she was free to come over and watch Jace, her heart would leap up, then instantly go into double-time.

There was no point in his hanging around, Asher thought. He was just wasting precious time. Time that Marnie's presence here was buying him.

"Okay, I'll be downstairs, working on the den," Asher murmured, leaving.

"We'll be right here," she called out after Asher. Turning toward Jace, she urged, "Okay, let's see that book of yours."

"It's right there." He pointed to the bookshelf on the far wall.

As she crossed the room with Jace, she debated whether or not to tell the boy that she was on to him. That she knew what his "master plan" was. Jace was acting like a holy terror so that his father would ask her to come over and keep him busy while he worked on whatever it was that needed doing that day. Once she arrived, Jace became an angel in her company. He behaved himself so that she wouldn't mind coming over.

That, to her, was some pretty advanced thinking for

a four-year-old. At ten, the boy would undoubtedly be a force to be reckoned with.

Right now Jace was, in effect, whether he knew it or not, her coconspirator in this, fixing it so that there was a reason for her to be here, to be around Asher, without it seeming to actually be her idea. Jace provided her with the excuse she needed to see his father.

So, for now, until the situation of Jace's acting out got to be too stressful for Asher, she decided to hold her tongue and just enjoy the company.

Both the boy's and his dad's.

With Marnie here to keep his son occupied, Asher knew he was free to get on with the overwhelming task of turning a two-story, newly constructed structure into an actual home.

His home.

But he was finding it harder and harder to concentrate on that work with Marnie so close by. He couldn't help thinking about a few minutes earlier, when he'd followed her and his son up the stairs. The view from his vantage point had been incredible.

The lyric out of some old country song flashed through his brain as he relived that tiny snippet of a recent memory. Something about hating to see a woman go, but, oh, to watch her leave.

He knew exactly what had been on the songwriter's mind. Watching Marnie walk up the stairs right in front of him was both a beautiful and stimulating sight.

Her jeans-clad hips had moved rhythmically, like wordless poetry.

It had taken him a moment to realize that he'd drawn in a breath, but hadn't let it out again. When he finally did, his heart had gone from double-time to racing.

He also realized, now that he thought about it, that he was calling Marnie more and more frequently, then asking her to stay for longer periods of time.

Initially, he really *had* tried to hold out, thinking that Jace would settle down, but now, at the first sign that the boy was about to act up, he was on the phone, calling Marnie to help. Feeling disappointed if he got her voice mail instead of her.

It wasn't so much that his patience was growing shorter or that his ability to cope was decreasing as it was that he was anticipating the pleasure of her company.

He had that in common with his son.

Because, inevitably, Jace would prevail upon her to stay for dinner.

The first time the boy had asked her, he'd been within earshot and heard her begin to demur. Pretending that he didn't want Jace to be disappointed, he'd raised his voice, seconding the boy's invitation. She'd laughed and said she was outnumbered, so she'd accept. After that, having her stay for dinner became almost a given.

Even so, Asher had a feeling that this would have to end soon. He knew that Marnie had to have better things to do than have dinner each night with the boy she babysat with and that boy's dad. A woman who looked like that—damn gorgeous even without a shred of makeup—had to have an active social life.

And yet she opted to spend her evenings here just to help him out.

Asher wasn't quite sure just how to repay her—money for her time didn't seem like nearly enough compensation. Moreover, he was at a loss as to how to have the situation continue.

Because he looked forward to her being here.

And that was the truth of it. He looked forward not just to having Jace act like the little boy he had been before Lynn had left them, but to having Marnie be part of their small inner circle.

Careful, Ash, he warned himself, *you're on dangerous ground here. You know what happens when you don't lead with your head.*

Yeah, he knew, but somehow, that didn't really seem to change anything.

Jace burst in on him a few hours later, beaming triumphantly and announcing, "Daddy, I got Marnie to stay for dinner again!"

Marnie was right behind him. Although she enjoyed the ritual, she also never took anything for granted. Just in case.

"You know the rules, Jace," she reminded him. "I'm only staying if it's okay with your dad."

Instead of waiting for his father to say something, the way he usually did, this time, Jace piped up, "Sure it's okay. He always says okay, don't you, Daddy?" he asked, turning to look up at his father.

Marnie looked over the boy's head, her eyes meeting Asher's.

"But he doesn't have to," she stipulated.

Just in case all this time Asher was being tolerant of this little game and her company at dinner, she wanted him to know that he wasn't obligated to invite her. That he had a choice.

She loved spending evenings here with the two of them, but she didn't want to force herself on Asher if he wanted some breathing space, or to spend some time alone with his son.

Or possibly even go out for the evening.

She realized that since she'd been coming over these last few weeks, Asher *hadn't* gone out in the evening. Nor had he asked her to babysit Jace while he escorted some woman who had caught his attention.

It surprised her just how much that fleeting thought pleased her.

"But he *wants* you to," Jace insisted, swinging around to look at his father again. "Don't you, Daddy?"

Asher smiled at his son and said what the boy was waiting to hear. "Yes, I do."

Was he just saying that, or did he actually mean that? Marnie couldn't help wondering. She knew what she *hoped* the answer to that was, but that definitely didn't make it so.

All she could do was smile at Asher brightly and tell him, "As long as you know that you have a way out. I do know my way home," she added as her smile traveled up to her eyes.

Did the woman have *any* idea how tempting her mouth looked when she smiled like that? Asher couldn't help wondering.

Looking at her right now, he could feel his gut tightening and all sorts of emotions beginning to run through his system, playing tug-of-war with his mind, with his libido and with just about everything else in between.

"Well, you don't have to find your way home quite yet," he told her.

Your way home.

The thought occurred to Marnie that she might already have found it.

Marnie stayed after dinner even longer than usual.

And this time, rather than clearing away the dishes with Jace and "allowing" him to help her stack them in the dishwasher, Marnie surprised both father and son by positioning a step stool in front of the sink. And then she proposed that they wash the dishes "the old-fashioned way."

Eager to do anything that pleased her, Jace asked, "What's that?"

"We put the dishes in the sink, fill it up with hot water and dishwashing liquid so that there are lots and lots of bubbles—and then we wash all the dishes, glasses and utensils by hand," she concluded, making it sound like a wonderful game.

Jace looked at her, completely taken with this "new" method. "Can we do that?" he wanted to know.

Biting back the laugh that rose in response to his question, she said, "We sure can. People did that before they had dishwashers."

His eyes were wide as he considered the scenario Marnie had painted. "When they were really poor, huh?" he asked.

Marnie draped an apron around his neck and tied it around his small waist, shoring it up as best she could. She had a feeling he was going to be pretty wet by the time this was over.

"Not poor, really," she answered. "They did it when they wanted to spend time talking to each other."

Jace's response was automatic. "Like you and me?" he asked eagerly.

Nothing got by this boy, she thought, delighted. "Exactly like you and me." She laughed.

Feeling that he'd looked on long enough, Asher came up to the sink and joined them. "Need someone to help dry?"

Humor instantly rose in her eyes as Marnie regarded Jace's father for a moment. If what she'd heard was true, Asher and his brothers were born with *two* silver spoons in their mouths, not just one. She was surprised he even knew where the sink was.

"Do you even know *how* to dry dishes?" she asked him.

Asher plucked a towel from the counter where she'd

placed it earlier this evening. "It's not exactly rocket science."

He wasn't answering her question directly. "So you've never actually done it before," she concluded with a grin.

"Wash something." Asher made it sound like a challenge.

Standing on the top of the step stool, Jace looked from Marnie to his father and then back again, his infectious smile seeming to grow larger by the moment.

"We're doing this together?" he wanted to know.

"It certainly looks that way," Marnie answered, trying hard not to show just how much this small, cozy scenario warmed her heart. "That is, if your dad can keep up."

"Keep up?" Asher echoed incredulously. His eyes narrowed as if he were an Olympic contender about to face his final round. "Bring it," he ordered her gamely, a dish towel in one hand, his other hand stretched out to her, waiting to be given the first clean, wet dish.

"Pick the first dish, Jace," she told the boy.

Sinking both his arms into the mountain of suds, Jace felt around and located a plate.

"Got one!" he declared, and then pulled it out of the water. Beaming, he handed it to her.

Without missing a beat, Marnie washed the dish quickly, front and back, then gave it to Asher, who deftly dried both sides of it and placed it on the counter next to him.

"Done," he declared in much the same way a calf

roper at a rodeo might say, stepping away from a trussed-up calf. "Next?"

Jace, who'd cheered on first Marnie, then his father as if this were some sort of marathon, clapped his hands together gleefully.

"This is fun, Marnie!" he declared. "You should move in with me and Daddy." Then added his closing argument, "'Cause daddies need mommies. And so do I."

Chapter Eight

A second later, in response to the boy's joyfully voiced suggestion and declaration, a deep blush rushed up Marnie's cheeks. She could literally *feel* it and deliberately avoided making any eye contact with Asher until she could feel her cheeks cooling again.

Even so, she was the one who recovered her tongue first.

"That is true, Jace," she told the four-year-old matter-of-factly. "You're absolutely right. Daddies *do* need mommies, just like mommies need daddies." Drying her hands, she cupped his little chin in her hand and tilted it slightly so that their eyes met. "But, honey, I'm not your mommy."

That apparently didn't represent an obstacle to him. "Would you like to be?" he asked eagerly, then added in a much sadder voice, "Mine went away and forgot all about me."

Marnie thought her heart was just going to break for the boy. She placed her hands on the boy's small, thin shoulders. "She didn't forget about you, Jace. Nobody could ever forget about someone like you." Wendy had told her about Asher's ex walking out on him, and she found herself really disliking the woman. But for Jace's sake, she painted a positive picture for him. "Your mom's just having trouble dealing with a few problems. Once she works them out, I know she'll try to get back in touch with you." She ran her fingers along his hair, stroking his head as she smiled into his eyes. "And someday, if I'm lucky enough to become a mommy, I hope that my little boy will be just like you."

Jace's smile was back, bigger and brighter than ever. "Really?"

"Really," she echoed with a nod. Wrapping her arms around the boy, she drew Jace to her and gave him a fierce hug.

"You are really something else, Jace Fortune," she told him. "But you're not really available, you know." She looked over toward Asher. "You belong to your dad."

Jace glanced back at his father, as if to make sure the man was still there in the kitchen. He guessed that they were a package deal, the way that man on the TV had said he was selling "two for the price of one."

"My dad's available, too," Jace told her in case she didn't know.

Okay, it was time to end this, Asher thought, before he was completely mortified.

"Time for bed," he announced, taking charge of Jace and quickly bringing an end to the exchange before his precocious son managed to get him into even more hot water.

"But we haven't finished the dishes yet," Jace protested, pointing to the sink.

"There's not that much left," Marnie assured him. "Don't worry, I'll take care of them."

The news was obviously not what Jace wanted to hear. "But then who's going to come upstairs with me and read me a story?" he wanted to know, looking directly at her.

Marnie glanced at the sink, then back at Jace. It wasn't even close. The boy won, hands down.

"I will," she told him, then added, "The dishes can wait. They're not going anywhere." She said the latter for Asher's benefit, just in case he thought she was running out on him after she'd made such a big deal out of washing everything by hand. "I'll do them before I leave," she promised.

If Asher heard her, he gave no indication. Instead, he took his son's hand. "Okay, let's go upstairs to your room, Jace."

But the boy twisted around so that he could look behind him at Marnie. "Marnie, too."

The boy was a born matchmaker, Asher thought, far less grudgingly than he would have initially expected himself to react to Jace's childish attempts to get him with a woman of his own choosing—which Marnie clearly was.

As a matter of fact, if he *had* to do his own choosing, Asher thought now, he would have picked someone who was pretty much like the woman his son had just grabbed by the hand and was currently urging toward the stairs.

Asher found himself walking behind her again.

And, just as before, he was treated to a view he found aesthetically pleasing. So much so that he actually hung back for a moment, utterly captivated and very close to being mesmerized.

You would have thought, he told himself a moment later, that he was some adolescent boy who hadn't completely gone through puberty yet. God knew he was too young to be experiencing a midlife crisis.

Just what the hell *was* going on with him?

Had Lynn walking out like that—getting involved with another man so quickly after the breakup—unmanned him to the point that he had to go through the whole maturation process again?

Or was it just a case, pure and simple, of being so utterly attracted to this woman that he found himself at a complete loss as to how to proceed, how to begin approaching her on some sort of a different plane than her being his son's sitter?

Coming to the landing, he glanced at his watch. It was getting kind of late, he realized. Not in the general scheme of things, but in the number of hours she had

already put in today. Ordinarily, Marnie stayed anywhere from three to six hours.

It was going on eight hours now.

He wasn't thinking of the amount of money he'd have
to pay her to reimburse her for her time. He could afford to pay her well over the price they had agreed to
when she had first begun babysitting Jace for him in
earnest. She was the one who said it was more than a
fair wage and that she wouldn't feel right taking more.

No, what he was afraid of was that he was wearing
Marnie out, that she just might one day tell him that
being here so long each day, making sure that Jace
didn't get into anything serious, was draining her.
Granted, the boy was on his best behavior around Marnie, but still, boys would be boys and his boy was a real
live wire even on his very best days.

"You don't have to do this, you know," he told Marnie as she got Jace ready for bed. "I can take it from
here if you want to go home."

Never missing a beat as she buttoned up the boy's
pajamas, she glanced up at Asher, smiled and serenely
said, "I know," then went right on getting Jace ready
for bed.

The last button slipped into the proper hole, she sat
back. "Okay, my man," she said, addressing the words
to Jace, unaware that her salutation had Asher abruptly
turn to look at her, "why don't you pick out the book
you'd like me to read to you tonight?"

"Yeah!"

Scrambling off the top of his comforter, he made a

beeline for his bookshelves, where he wound up picking out a book entitled *Freddie Gets Ready*.

"Interesting choice," she observed, waiting for the boy to get back into the bed. Tucking Jace in, she began to read.

Freddie, it turned out, was a baby dragon and what he was getting ready for, she discovered as she read the story to Jace with all the drama and voice shifts that belonged to a major melodrama, was his first day at kindergarten.

Reading it, Marnie couldn't help wondering if Jace had deliberately picked the book to help him face the same rite of passage in a few months.

She would have asked him when she came to the end of the story, but when she closed the book Jace had fallen sound asleep.

Smiling, she tucked the covers around him a little more closely, bent over the sleeping boy and lightly brushed her lips against his forehead. Jace shifted suddenly, murmured something and seemed to smile.

Turning, Marnie began to tiptoe out of the room. The very next second, she stifled a gasp when she realized she wasn't alone. Asher was standing in the doorway, watching her.

Recovering quickly, she crossed to the doorway, then walked by Asher and out of the room.

When he followed, easing the door closed behind him, she swung around to face him and asked, "How long were you standing there?"

There was no hesitation. "Long enough to know that

Freddie was going to have a good first day at kinder-garten," he told her with a smile.

Watching her read to Jace had really gotten to him. In all the time that Lynn had forced herself to remain in her son's life, she'd never once read to the boy, even though Jace had asked her to. Asher had seen more ten-derness displayed toward Jace in this single day than Lynn had managed to show their son during the entire time she'd lived with them.

Asher sighed. He supposed that it took more than giving birth and donating genes to be a mother.

"That was nice," he told Marnie.

She didn't quite follow his meaning. Was he talk-ing about Freddie's being happy at the end? "Do you mean the story?"

"No, I mean you reading it to him," he corrected. "Jace really responds to you." Anyone could see that, but for now, he was just going to enjoy that and not overthink the situation.

"He's a little boy," she pointed out in case Asher's feelings were secretly hurt because it appeared that his son preferred her to him. "He'd respond to anyone giving him a little attention, making him feel as if he counted. But I've watched him. He clearly loves you," she emphasized.

"I know that." Even if, at times, Jace drove him ab-solutely crazy, he never doubted the boy's love. "I also know how hurt he was when Lynn walked out. Because of you, he's put that behind him. Thanks for making my son forget about the pain he felt."

She didn't want to contradict him, but Asher needed to be aware of something. "Oh, I think he'll remember for quite a while."

He supposed that she was right, and that weighed heavily on him. Had he let Lynn go right after the boy had been born, Jace would never have missed his mother because he would never have *known* his mother.

"Yes, I know," he agreed, "but it'll have less of a sting with you around."

She smiled at the way Asher had phrased that. "So, is that your way of saying that you're keeping me on?"

"Keeping you on?" he repeated with an incredulous laugh. "I'm ready to adopt you if it meant you'd go on being around—for Jace," he added quickly, afraid that maybe he'd said too much, given her the wrong impression—or maybe, he amended, the right one, but one that she probably didn't want.

"Jace didn't have that bad an idea," Asher went on, groping his way through a conversation that he was basically winging from the very start.

He wasn't good at this, he couldn't help thinking. He'd always been a man who was good with his hands, not with the words coming out of his mouth.

"And which idea was that?" she asked, trying to coax a conversation out of the man. He was very much the strong, silent type, she thought. That had its place, too, but right now she craved a good conversation.

"About you moving in."

He saw her eyes widen and realized his mistake.

Quick, you're scaring her off. Do something. Say

something. Something smart for a change, he amended angrily.

"As his nanny, I mean," Asher blurted out.

"As his nanny," she repeated slowly.

Was he making a point of that because he was afraid she might get other ideas—or was *he* the one getting other ideas?

And if so, just what kind of ideas was he getting?

He was waiting for an answer, she realized. And his question opened up a whole bunch of other considerations. Ones she didn't just disregard lightly.

"Let me get back to you on that," she finally told him.

There was nothing in her voice, one way or another, to indicate whether she was going to take him up on it, or if she even liked the suggestion.

Or had he just insulted her?

When Marnie turned away, he had a sinking feeling that he *had* scared her off.

Stepping up his pace, he caught her by the arm to get her to turn around again and face him. But in so doing, he caused her to drop the book she was holding.

A book until this second she didn't realize she was still holding. She'd walked off with the storybook she'd just finished reading to Jace.

She bent down quickly to pick the book up, wanting to return it to his shelves. Asher had the same idea as she did.

The upshot was they wound up bumping heads and nearly knocking each other over.

Embarrassed, a sliver of pain piercing through his

head, his hand darted out to steady Marnie and keep her from falling backward.

Succeeding in doing both, Asher rose to his feet, still holding her wrist. Marnie was forced to get to her feet right along with him.

Looking up at Asher as they stood closer than two shadows at midnight, she felt a rush of heat a hundred-fold hotter than what she'd felt in her cheeks when Jace had unintentionally suggested she become his mommy.

Her breath caught in her throat and she couldn't have made the tiniest move unless the earth picked that moment to open up beneath her feet.

Driven by forces that were timeless and far stronger than he was, Asher gave in to the longing that had been his constant companion from the moment he had laid eyes on her.

Certainly from the moment she had walked into his house.

He really had no clear conception of how he went from point A to point B, from looking down into her face to kissing her lips.

All he knew was that he did.

And when he did, all hell seemed to break loose inside him.

Suddenly, just like that, as his lips pressed against hers and he felt a spirited, invigorating force spreading out all through him, the loneliness that had haunted him for the last six months dissolved.

The kiss deepened. Asher filled his hands with her hair, lightly pressing his fingertips against the back of her head as he absorbed sensations he'd been so sure he'd never experience again. It all contributed to the growing feeling of well-being he could feel radiating within him.

Chapter Nine

*D*on't, Marnie warned herself even as she felt herself being engulfed. *Don't. He won't want you to keep coming over if he thinks you have feelings for him.*

Stop!

But none of the words echoing in her brain had any effect on Marnie.

She went on kissing him.

And her heart went on singing.

A moment later, the song Marnie heard playing in her head abruptly stopped.

Asher had suddenly drawn back away from her, ending the spectacular kiss they were sharing and with it, the magical moment, as well.

What the hell was he doing? a voice in his head demanded.

Now that his life was finally taking on some shape, some order, did he really want to sacrifice all that because he *thought* he felt something for this woman? *Thought* he was attracted to her?

He'd been that route before—and turned out to be dead wrong.

Okay, Marnie was definitely beautiful in a warm, approachable way, but was he reacting to Marnie because he was lonely and it had been such a very long time since he'd actually *been* with a woman?

Or was his reaction governed by his feelings of gratitude and tremendous relief that his son was behaving himself, thanks to her presence and influence, allowing him to have a little breathing space and get a few things done rather than exclusively devoting himself twenty-four/seven to the boy?

Asher felt he wasn't clearheaded enough right now to be able to hone in on the real reason that was responsible for what had just taken place. All Asher *did* know was that for the first time in years, he'd felt both a peacefulness and a warm glow within him just now when he'd held Marnie in his arms and kissed her.

Be that as it may, that still didn't excuse his rash action. She was his babysitter, for God's sake, not his girlfriend.

And right now she was looking at him with confusion in her expressive brown eyes.

"Sorry," Asher murmured, his voice so low it was all but inaudible. "I didn't mean to do that."

"Oh." Marnie continued looking at him and then,

a second later, she took a step backward, away from him, saying, "Then I guess I'd better take a step or two back from you."

Asher didn't understand the connection she was making. "Why?"

The expression on her face was innocence personified. "Because your nose is going to start growing any second now and I don't want to get in its way. It might get painful."

"My—what?" His eyebrow all but knit together in an expressive, long, wavy line as he stared at her, completely lost.

"Your nose," she repeated. Ever so slowly, the innocent look receded, to be replaced by an expression that had a glimmer of mischief to it. "You know, like Pinocchio in the fairy tale. Whenever he lied, his nose would automatically start growing." Marnie pretended to stare at his nose, waiting. "I suspect that yours will, too, any second now."

Maybe he should have been insulted, Asher thought, but instead, he found himself being amused. "You're telling me you think I'm lying?"

Marnie nodded and solemnly repeated, "I'm telling you I think you're lying."

He could feel the corners of his mouth curving as the tension he'd felt only moments ago began to drain away. "And why's that?"

That was a simple enough question to answer, she thought. "You forget, I was on the other side of that 'involuntary' kiss, and from where I stood, it certainly didn't feel as if you just suddenly tripped and tried to break your fall with your lips."

Since she was taking what had happened so well, Asher decided he owed it to her to be honest. "I don't want to do anything that would cause you not to come back tomorrow. Jace would never forgive me if that happened."

She nodded slowly, as if giving his answer due consideration, instead of telling him that what he'd just said was ridiculous.

"I can think of maybe a handful of things you could do to keep me from coming back," she told Asher. "*None* of which include what just happened here tonight," she emphasized.

Time, and dealing with Lynn, had taught him to proceed cautiously and make sure all his *i*'s were dotted and his *t*'s were crossed.

Looking into her eyes, he asked, "So you're not offended?"

Under the circumstances—and the fact that she had definitely kissed back—she found that a very strange word for him to use.

"You kissed me, Asher. You didn't stand in the town square and denounce me before God and country or call me a whole bunch of names that would completely blacken my character." She shook her head. What kind of a witch had his ex-wife been, to rob Asher this way of his confidence and self-esteem? "My God, Asher, if I'm out of line here, just tell me, but it seems to me like

Jace's mother must have been some piece of work for you to be this unsure of yourself."

Marnie was even more intuitive than he'd thought. Also more outspoken. By the time Lynn had finally left, his ego and everything else about him had felt as if it was in tatters.

"You're not out of line," he told her, "but I'd really rather not talk about it."

"Understood," she told him. The topic was probably too painful for him to relive, and she could accept that. She'd had breakups in her past that she would rather not talk about, too. She could just imagine how much worse it had to have been to go through the breakup of a marriage. "I'll drop it. But I think you should go out of your way to reassure your son that he *is* lovable and that his mother walking out on the two of you was in no way his fault."

Asher surprised her by suddenly taking hold of her arm and drawing her down the stairs, going as far away from his son's bedroom door as possible.

Only when they were practically standing by the front door did he finally say what he wanted to tell her.

"For the most part, it was my fault, but what finally drove Lynn away was that she just didn't want to be a mother."

And that, she could see, could be interpreted as technically being Jace's fault, that he *was* the reason his mother had left.

She searched Asher's face to see if he actually did

blame the boy and was relieved to discover that he really didn't.

She found herself *really* disliking a woman she had never met.

"Not every woman is cut out to be a mother," Marnie pointed out simply.

"It was my fault," he repeated. "I forced her."

He was really beating himself up about this breakup, she thought. The desire to help him get past this only grew.

"You held a gun to her head and said, have my baby or else?" she deadpanned.

She made him laugh despite himself. "No, but when she told me she was pregnant and wanted to 'take care of the matter,'" he said, quoting the euphemism Lynn had used, "I begged her not to. I asked her to marry me and have the baby."

She just had one question for him. "Did you ask her to marry you because of her or because of the baby?"

"Both." He'd been greedy and wanted both. Lynn *and* the baby.

Either answer would have been good enough. What he said, in her opinion, was stellar.

"Well, either way, you have no reason to fault yourself, and since it's both, that erases any fault twice over. You did the 'right' thing, the noble thing. And, from what I've gathered from the bits and pieces I've put together since I've been coming over here, you kept on doing it for over three years." Which, all things con-

sidered, made him one of the most patient men she had
ever met.

"Lynn tried hard," he said, feeling obligated to defend the woman who had finally walked out on him, on
their son, without so much as a backward glance. He
had to give her her due, he thought. It was only right.
"She tried for three years, until she just couldn't try
anymore." Maybe it *was* all his fault. He didn't know
anymore. "I shouldn't have forced her," he concluded
quietly.

For a moment, Marnie debated holding her tongue.
After all, Asher's actions, his feelings about his life,
were his own business. But she wanted him not to lose
sight of one very important point.

Her silence lasted less than thirty seconds.

"Maybe," she allowed, "but if you hadn't talked her
into having the baby, that boy sleeping upstairs wouldn't
be here right now, and personally, I think that would
have been a huge loss for you."

She was right, he thought. He couldn't imagine life
without Jace. Still, "Jace wears me out," he told her with
more than a touch of weariness.

"True." She could see that the boy was a handful,
even if he was on his best behavior with her. "But he
also makes you smile. I've seen it. I think, ultimately,
while your ex-wife wasn't meant to be a mother, you
were definitely meant to be a father. There's a bond between you and Jace. Anyone can see that. And whether
you want to admit it or not, your life would be very
empty now without him."

She had insight, he'd give her that.

Asher could feel himself smiling even though he wanted to appear solemn for at least a second longer. "And what makes you such an authority?"

She laughed then, her eyes shining with humor. "Haven't you heard? I'm very wise."

Asher looked at her for a long moment. "Yes," he said without a trace of humor in his tone, "you are."

If he didn't let her go now, Asher thought, he never would.

Forcing himself to open the door for her, he said, "Well, it's late and Jace and I have kept you far too long today. I really appreciate all your help—and your pep talk," he added.

Marnie crossed the threshold and then turned around to look at him one last time before she drove away. "Did it do any good? The pep talk?" She wanted to know.

"Yeah," he answered honestly, "it did." He forced himself to stay where he was; otherwise who knew how long they would linger on the front step? "You'll be back tomorrow?"

She nodded, then pretended to qualify her reply. "Unless one of the horses runs off with me."

He took her answer in the spirit that it was given. "One way to prevent that. Keep your feet on the ground," he advised.

Marnie nodded again as she finally took her leave. "I'll try to remember that."

But it was actually too late for that, she added silently. His kiss had seen to that.

* * *

Marnie bolted upright, her eyes wide open and staring. Seeing nothing.

She was still caught halfway between reality and a netherworld composed of dreams.

The darkness around her slowly penetrated as she forced herself to focus.

She was in her room.

It was still somewhere in the middle of the night. The promise of sunlight wasn't even a glimmer yet.

She'd been dreaming, but was now awake. Awake and in a puddle of sweat.

Just as she had been last night and the night before that.

And the night before that.

The dreams were all different, but the same. The settings varied, as did the beginnings, but they *all* took the same path, all wound up the same way.

This one had been the most realistic yet.

When the dreams had first begun a little more than a week ago, she knew she was dreaming while it was happening. And she was also aware of why she was having this particular kind of dream.

Because she was attracted to Asher and could do in her dreams what she couldn't do in real life.

But as the dreams took on more depth, more dimension, more detail, she began to have trouble separating them from reality. They seemed to be so very, very real that while she was having them, it was as if she was actually living in the moment.

In each one of the dreams, she and Asher went from talking, to touching, to kissing. The end would abruptly come when they began getting really physical. She'd wake up then with a start, damp with perspiration and restless with longings that had ultimately gone unfulfilled.

And each night, they went a little further in the scenario created by her mind. Each night, a little more happened.

And tonight, tonight Asher had almost taken her completely before her brain had called a halt to it, pulling the plug so to speak and forcing her into a wakeful state.

Marnie realized that her pulse was still racing and that she was still very breathless.

She was actually breathless, she marveled. What was going on with her?

Was she going crazy?

The source of this last accelerated step was definitely not a mystery. She knew what had triggered it. Asher's kiss last night had given her something *real* to build on in her dream.

Marnie pulled her knees up to her chest, laced her arms around them and then rested her head against the arch that was formed.

She couldn't go on like this.

Couldn't go on dreaming about Asher every night. If nothing else, she wasn't getting enough sleep. She couldn't afford to be moving around like some bleary-eyed zombie as she went through her day. She needed to be the exact opposite—at the top of her game—when she turned up at work at Coventry.

Not that she thought anything would happen to the riding students she taught, but just the vague possibility that it might was enough to put fear into her heart. The last thing she wanted was to risk someone getting hurt because she was having exotic dreams that left her yearning for fulfillment.

So what were her options?

She could quit babysitting for Asher, she supposed. But that didn't mean that she would automatically stop having those dreams. The man with his dimpled grin was still very much in her mind and could quite possibly stay there for a very long time. She couldn't remember the last time she'd reacted so strongly to a man. And as for dreaming about a man, well, that had never happened before.

And besides, if she quit, that would leave Asher in a very bad way and she'd really miss Jace. Not to mention that having *two* women he had been emotionally tied to leaving him would be devastating to the little boy's self-esteem as well as his budding ego. She just couldn't do that to the boy *or* his father.

Another option, she supposed, was just getting this overwhelming longing—because that was what it was at bottom—out of her system. That meant going up to Asher, saying that they were both adults and obviously attracted to each other so they should just go ahead and sleep together as a way of getting all that sexual tension out of the way.

"Right, really romantic, Marnie," she upbraided herself. "Not to mention really stupid. I don't care what other women are doing these days," she argued. "You're not propositioning Asher Fortune just so you can get a good night's sleep again."

Okay, now she was arguing with herself. This was getting serious, she thought as a touch of desperation shot through her.

Marnie dragged one hand through her hair, trying to think of a third alternative.

None readily suggested itself.

She could, she supposed, just try to wait it out. Wait out these soul-melting, mind-bending erotic dreams. Eventually, her brain had to move on to something else, right?

Or just blank out.

Before this X-rated spate of dreams had hit, she hadn't had *any* dreams while she slept—or at least none that she was aware of—for several years. It was a matter of closing her eyes and then, before she knew it, it was time to get up again.

All the hours in between were pleasantly, restfully blank.

She wanted that back again, she thought, shifting in her bed as she reached for her pillow.

The side she'd been sleeping on was really damp with sweat.

Marnie sighed, shaking her head, then flipped the pillow over to its other side.

If this kept up and she continued having these "almost but not quite" dreams, she was going to have to stake herself to some brand-new pillows and bedclothes, she thought.

"Now, there's a novel reason to go shopping for new sheets," she said out loud to the darkness.

Punching the pillow a couple of times as she tried to find a comfortable spot for herself, Marnie lay down again.

But rather than fall asleep, she merely started shifting restlessly from side to side.

Exhausted, but still too leery of what might be waiting for her just ahead in the misty land of dreams, she continued to lie there, awake and staring at her darkened ceiling.

She wondered if self-hypnosis would help and just how to go about doing it if it could.

She was still wondering as dawn finally began seeping into the room.

And then she fell asleep.

Chapter Ten

Gloria McCafferty silently appraised her only daughter the next morning when Marnie, still somewhat bleary-eyed, made her way into the kitchen.

Frowning to herself, the older woman shook her head. "Well, you look like hell," she said, not without some concern.

Marnie went straight to the coffee machine and poured herself a full cup of steaming coffee. "Thank you, Mother," she replied only after taking her first long, life-affirming sip of the brew. "And good morning to you, too."

Gloria sighed to herself as she placed a serving of scrambled eggs and toast—Marnie's favorite—in front of her daughter.

Anyone looking at the mother felt as if they were

getting a preview of what the daughter would look like in another two decades. They had the same light brown hair—Gloria wore hers shorter—and the same chocolate-brown, expressive eyes.

And right now Gloria's eyes were not pleased.

The landlord of the apartment building Marnie had been living in until two months ago had suddenly announced that the building was going co-op. Unable to find new living quarters immediately—or come up with the down payment necessary to buy in to the apartment she'd been happily living in for the last four years—Marnie had reluctantly opted to temporarily move back in with her mother.

She'd done it more or less in self-defense. After her mother had initially extended the invitation, she'd prefaced each conversation they'd had with a strongly voiced invitation until Marnie had agreed to the arrangement out of exhaustion.

Temporarily, she'd emphasized.

It wasn't that she didn't love her mother; she did. Dearly. But there was nothing that made her feel as if she was twelve years old again faster than living in her mother's house and sleeping in her old bedroom with her old teddy bear looking down on her from his perch atop the bookcase.

"I thought I heard you arguing with someone last night," Gloria said, deciding the direct approach was the best one to use rather than looking for a subtle way to broach the subject.

She took a seat across from her daughter at the

kitchen table, her coffee mug serving as a place holder. "Who were you talking to?" she wanted to know.

"Nobody," Marnie answered. Her mother continued eyeing her skeptically. The woman had missed her calling, Marnie thought. She should be been an interrogator for some law-enforcement agency. She would undoubtedly have made a good one. "I guess I must have been talking in my sleep," she finally added, hoping that was enough to table the matter.

She should have known better.

"Sounded extremely coherent for talking in your sleep," Gloria commented. "Sure you weren't on the phone with that man?"

It was Marnie's turn to frown. She had no idea what her mother was talking about. "What man?"

"That *man*," Gloria repeated, stressing the second word, as if that would unlock the puzzle. "You know, the father of that little boy you were telling me about. The one you're always going over to babysit for until all hours."

"I came home late only once, Mother," Marnie pointed out. "Yesterday." She leveled a look at the woman. They had an agreement, or at least she thought they had. "You know how I feel about you 'tracking' me. I only agreed to stay here until I found a new place because you promised not to treat me as if I was still in high school." She issued both a request and a plea, all rolled up into one. "Stop worrying about me, Mom."

"I'm your mother," Gloria protested. "I'm supposed to worry about you. It's built into my DNA, which said that I would have large bones, love all forms of ice cream and worry about my daughter as long as she remains single. Trust me, it's in the bylaws."

Marnie pinned her mother with a long, exasperated look. "What bylaws?"

"The mother-daughter bylaws," Gloria answered simply. "Now eat before it all gets cold."

That, at least, was not a hardship. She absolutely loved her mother's cooking. Her mother had the ability to turn a simple serving of eggs and toast into a veritable feast.

Gloria smiled as she watched her daughter do justice to the breakfast she'd made for her. "There's a provision in those bylaws that says if my daughter has a habit of falling for strays, I'm allowed to worry about her—and you know you have a habit of falling for men who 'need' you. Like that last one—"

Marnie could tell by the tone her mother was using that she was getting all wound up. Marnie was quick to hold up her hand to stop what she knew would be an absolute deluge of words—all at her expense.

That was absolutely the *last* thing she needed to hear right now.

"Let's just table that discussion for now, Mom." Even so, she couldn't resist making one final point. "In my defense, I really did think that Luke was the one."

Gloria had lost five pounds, worrying, when Marnie and Luke had been together. "And Luke really thought you were his own personal ATM."

If she had one outstanding fault, Marnie thought, it was that she was an extremely soft touch.

"Lesson learned, Mother." The words were said through gritted teeth, which served as a definite warning note of itself. It was meant to tell her mother to back off. Now. "Besides, Asher isn't like that."

"No, this one comes equipped with his own kid, your own personal weakness. The only thing worse would have been if the kid came with his own pony, making the whole thing a trifecta," Gloria concluded, sighing dramatically for Marnie's benefit.

She didn't expect Marnie to laugh.

But Marnie couldn't help herself.

"Asher Fortune is *not* a stray, Mother," Marnie informed. "Besides, he *pays* me to keep his energetic son occupied while he gets settled in. We have a working relationship, that's all."

Either her daughter was being naive or she was shutting her out, Gloria thought. Neither explanation pleased her.

"Is it?" Gloria asked, eyeing her again.

"Yes!" Marnie retorted a little too emphatically.

"Maybe you've fooled yourself into believing that," Gloria granted, "but you can't fool me. I know you too well, Marnie. You have a heart as big as all outdoors. This Asher person is broken and you're trying to fix him. It's in your nature, honey." Gloria sighed, putting down her coffee mug. "I just don't want you getting hurt again, that's all. You have a big heart and that's a lovely thing, really. But when that big heart causes you to get hurt, time and time again, well, then I just—"

"I've hardened that heart, Mother," Marnie informed her abruptly. She wrapped up the last of the toast in her napkin and rose. "I'd love to sit and continue talking about my late, lamented love life with you, but that'll make me *really* late for work and I'm already running behind."

Rounding the table, Marnie paused to brush her lips against her mother's cheek. "Thanks for caring, Mom," she said, the edge in her voice gone for the moment.

Gloria patted her hand. "Just promise you'll be careful, okay?"

"Okay," Marnie responded, not really sure just what her mother meant by that or exactly what she should be careful about, but it was still nice to know that she had someone who cared about her enough to say that.

If only her mother didn't care *quite* so much, Marnie couldn't help thinking as she raced up the stairs to her room, to finish getting dressed.

She supposed, Marnie thought as she hurried into her clothes and applied her sparse makeup in record time, that her mother did have a point—a *minor* point, she silently emphasized. She *did* seem to have a weakness for anyone who came across as lost and hurt, two words that could also aptly be applied to Asher.

That glimpse he'd allowed her to have into his past last night definitely placed the man among the walking wounded. And she *did* have a tendency to want to make the pain go away.

Was there more to the story, or had his marriage really ended because his wife just couldn't handle being a mother to a demanding child?

There was absolutely no doubt in her mind that Jace could be a real handful and a half to deal with. If Asher's ex had had trouble getting the boy to mind her or to settle down when she wanted him to, Marnie could see how that could be frustrating.

But frustrating enough to walk out on the whole package deal?

Marnie shook her head. She just couldn't wrap her mind around something like that. She knew that no matter how angry they would get her, she would *never* abandon her children.

If she ever got to the stage where she was lucky enough to have them in the first place, Marnie amended.

All day long, her mind kept coming back to what Asher had told her last night.

Had he told her the full story about the breakup, or were there parts that he'd "conveniently" omitted? And if so, why? And, equally important, what were they?

There was no point in denying that she was attracted to him, and she was fairly certain after last night that he was attracted to her, as well, but was her mother right? *Was* Asher just another stray, except in expensive clothing, looking to her to help him heal or fix whatever it was that was wrong?

Her head was filled with questions, and there were absolutely no readily applicable answers anywhere in the near vicinity.

Stop it, she ordered herself. *You're overthinking this and you're going to make yourself crazy and* then *where will you be? You certainly won't be able to watch Jace or be there for his dad if you're a certifiable nutcase.*

She needed a break, Marnie decided. A break from her routine.

Maybe a night out with an old girlfriend she hadn't seen for a while would get her back on track, Marnie thought.

The next second, as her last student of the day dismounted and led her horse back to the stable, to groom the mare before putting her away, Marnie took out her cell phone.

She knew exactly whom to call.

As luck would have it, her girlfriend turned out to be free that evening. Plans were solidified.

"Well, this is really nice, getting together for dinner and a movie like this," Nicole Castleton commented over her plate of well-done barbecued spareribs. "Although I must say I was surprised to hear from you out of the blue like that. How long has it been now?" she wanted to know.

Marnie thought for a moment. "A couple of months or so," she guessed, not really able to pin down the last time the two of them had gone out together. There just never seemed to be enough hours in the day.

Nicole Castleton had been her very best friend in high school. Back then, they had been close to insepa-rable despite the fact that they couldn't have come from two more different backgrounds. While Marnie came from working-class roots, Nicole was a child of privilege even though she didn't behave that way.

Or at least, she didn't flaunt the fact that her family was more than just well-to-do.

Initially, Marnie and Nicole had bonded over their mutual interest in horses and boys, not necessarily in that order.

These days, when they did manage to see each other, the topic always turned to the fact that they both felt that a good man was next to impossible to find.

You had to kiss a lot of frogs before you found your prince was the way Marnie had once put it, but as far as Nicole was concerned, she'd already kissed her prince. Kissed him and then lost him, all while still in high school.

Though her friend would deny it, Marnie suspected that Nicole compared every new man she met to her old high school sweetheart. Compared them and found them all to be lacking, which was why a girl as beautiful as Nicole was still very much alone.

Marnie, on the other hand, always tended to find too many attributes—usually imagined and not real—in the man of the moment.

But at least she'd been trying.

Maybe trying too hard, she thought the next moment as her mother's voice seemed to echo in her head, cautioning her about taking in "strays."

"So, tell me about Jace's dad," Nicole coaxed suddenly. She saw the surprise in Marnie's face. "Hey, it's a small town, Marn, remember? Word gets around. Fast."

"What kind of word?" Marnie asked suspiciously. Gossips thought nothing of fabricating a thing or two and adding it to an existing rumor, padding it just for effect.

Marnie held her breath as her friend answered her question.

"You know, that he's handsome, kind and he's a Fortune, which means he comes from good people and really nice money," she added with a wide grin. "You ask me, he sounds perfect."

Actually, he was, Marnie thought. But it wouldn't be right to carry on about Asher, not when Nicole was currently between candidates whom she would ultimately reject. So, to spare her friend's feelings, Marnie said, "Maybe not so perfect. After all, his ex-wife walked out on him."

That certainly didn't sound like a deterrent to Nicole. "So? Go comfort the poor man." She grinned as she paused to take a sip of her drink. "C'mon, Marnie, what have you got to lose? Take a chance. He just might be the one."

That was her line, Marnie couldn't help thinking. To her surprise, for some reason she found herself making noises like her mother in response. "Maybe, but he's got to make the first move."

Now, that surprised Nicole. "You mean—he hasn't done anything?"

"Well, he did kiss me," Marnie admitted, ready to

place a disclaimer on the event that had heated up the very blood in her veins.

But Nicole never gave her the chance to say anything, because as soon as Marnie told her that Asher had kissed her, Nicole triumphantly declared, "Aha!" And then she looked more closely at her friend. Marnie did *not* look thrilled to death. "Honey, if you don't want him, just toss the man my way. I know just what to do to put a smile on his face."

To which Marnie cautioned, "Not so fast, Nic."

That only made Nicole grin broadly. "I thought you might change your mind. This kiss, when did it happen?"

"Last night."

The admission startled Nicole.

She stared at Marnie in disbelief. "Last night? Then what are you doing here with me? Why aren't you over at his place, trying to appear casual when you're really waiting for Act Two?"

Now Marnie was really lost. "Act Two?"

"Obviously you're a newbie in these matters—either that or you just haven't been paying attention," Nicole teased. "All right, I'll go over it for you. The hero breaks the ice in Act One. Act Two is when the *real* action takes place. Wait, you didn't push him away and act all indignant, did you?"

Pushing Asher away was just about the last thing in the world she would have wanted to do. "No, it was very sweet, really."

"And that's all?" Nicole asked, disappointed.

Marnie knew what her friend was waiting for. Details. "Also incredibly passionate and damn near bone-melting."

Nicole smiled, letting her imagination go. "That's better. Okay, dinner and a movie are officially canceled," she declared, putting her fork down and raising her hand to catch the waiter's attention. "We're leaving and you're getting back on that horse, my friend."

Had Nicole always talked in riddles this way, or was that something that had occurred just recently? "Horse? What horse?"

"The one that figuratively threw you *Asher Fortune,* for God's sake. Do I have to spell out everything for you? I think your kissing him scared you—"

"*He* kissed *me,*" Marnie corrected.

Nicole was not about to be thrown off the track she was on. "And you kissed him back, right?"

"Yes," Marnie almost grudgingly admitted, knowing that Nicole would just run amok with the implications behind a mutual kiss. She hadn't settled the matter to her satisfaction in her own head yet, and the last thing she wanted was to have Nicole start giving her this annoying, *knowing* look.

But for once Nicole surprised her. "So get back there and do it again. Do it for me if not for yourself."

"For you," Marnie repeated, amused and bemused at the same time.

"Hey, I'm living vicariously here. Besides, if you decide that Asher Fortune really isn't right for you, the guy's gonna be twice as vulnerable as he supposedly is right now," Nicole told her. "Don't ask me how I know that he's vulnerable. I know you. Those are the kinds of guys you're attracted to—and I get to swoop in to the rescue."

Nicole smiled beatifically as the waiter approached. "Check please," she told him. Turning to Marnie for a second, she interjected, "My treat—don't argue," in the form of an order. "And hurry." This last instruction was meant for the young waiter with the trim hips. "My friend here has a man to catch."

Nicole seemed completely oblivious of the mortified but dirty look that Marnie was giving her.

Chapter Eleven

"When's Marnie going to get here, Daddy?" Jace wanted to know. He shifted impatiently from foot to foot as he quizzed his father.

The child had been alternating between moping and having occasional spurts of unfocused, disruptive energy. So far, the casualties—a drinking glass and an old vase Asher had never really cared for—had been minor. But he knew that he was by no means out of the woods as far as the matter of accidental breakage went until Jace was finally down for the night and sound asleep.

Right now that, too, seemed pretty much like an unattainable dream to him.

"She's busy tonight, Jace," he told his son, saying it as if it were new information and he hadn't already said the very same thing to him possibly a dozen times during the long course of the day, except that the word *today* had been used instead of *tonight* at the time.

"Busy?" Jace echoed in childish disbelief. "She's *still* busy? Busy doing what?" he wanted to know, his impatience clearly escalating.

Dinner had been pretty much a disaster, both the preparation and the subsequent consummation, neither of which had been satisfactorily achieved.

Asher felt as if he was really beginning to run out of patience himself.

Turning to his son, he placed his hands on the boy's shoulders, holding him still as he addressed the question. Again.

"Marnie *does* have a life outside of us, buddy. She was teaching her riding students this morning, and as for tonight, she called and said something about having dinner with a friend and then going to the movies."

If he were being truthful with himself, Asher had to admit he wasn't overly thrilled with the excuse, either, except that in his case, he found himself wondering if this "friend," whom Marnie hadn't identified by name or gender, was actually some man who was taking her out on a date.

Ever since she'd mentioned it to him over the phone today, he'd been dealing with conflicting emotions. There were definite strains of jealousy battling with his insistence that he had no right to be jealous, that he really wasn't ready to undertake any sort of a relationship yet, especially since his last one had been nothing short of a raging failure.

But that didn't stop him from feeling like this, and Jace's restlessness was *not* helping the matter.

"When will *that* be over?" Jace wanted to know with a giant sigh.

Asher knew where his son was going with this. He tried to nip it in the bud. "Too late for her to come over tonight."

The answer was *not* acceptable to the unhappy little boy. "But she *has* to come over. I can't go to sleep unless she reads me a story."

Jace made it sound as if it were a nightly ritual and Marnie was skipping out on it. The kid did have a flair for drama, Asher couldn't help thinking.

"Once," he pointed out to the boy. "She did that once. You went to sleep all those other nights without her, remember? I was the one who read you the stories. Does she read stories so much better than I do?" he asked, trying to get the boy to see reason.

He should have known better.

"Yes," Jace answered bluntly without any hesitation whatsoever.

So much for the boy growing up to be in the diplomatic corps. "Good thing my feelings don't get hurt easily," Asher quipped.

Jace seemed to be oblivious of the effect his comment had on his father. He was only focused on one thing. "I want Marnie. Please?" the boy added with a quivering lip. "Call her, Daddy. Call her for me," he pleaded. "Tell her I want her to come over."

Asher supposed that he could put his foot down and

flat-out say, "No," but he knew damn well that Jace was not about to give up. This little back-and-forth thing had the markings of something that could go on *all* night.

So he decided to try to strike a bargain with the boy instead.

"Okay, I'll call her," he said to Jace, "but if I do, even if she says she can't come, you have to go to bed." He looked directly into his son's eyes. "Deal?"

The boy thought for a moment, then had a counteroffer to give him. Asher had expected nothing less. "Can I be the one to talk to her?"

"All right, but just to say good night." He knew that most parents would have said that he was surrendering, but he was fairly confident that the call would go straight to voice mail. He'd still get Jace to bed per their agreement, and this way, he wouldn't be the bad guy.

"Then deal," the boy agreed. He cocked his head, waiting. "Are you gonna call her number now?"

The sooner this was out of the way, the sooner he'd get Jace upstairs and to bed, he told himself. It had been a *really* long day.

"Sure, why not? As long as you promise to honor our deal."

"I promise," Jace said solemnly.

"Okay, I'm taking you at your word," Asher told his son.

Taking out his cell phone, he tapped out Marnie's number on his keypad. Halfway through the procedure, Asher realized that he didn't have to look her number up. Apparently, it was etched into his brain.

He told himself it was only because he'd called her so often, asking her to come over and watch Jace, *not* because she was preying on his mind, lingering there like a melody that refused to go away.

The call, as he'd predicted, went straight to voice mail. As she told whoever was calling to please leave a message, Asher held the phone out to his son so he could hear Marnie's voice.

It wasn't that he thought his son doubted him so much as he found Jace to be possibly the most cautious four-year-old on record.

Taking hold of the cell phone with both hands, Jace made his plea. "Marnie, you gotta come over. I can't go to sleep unless you read a story to me." As he concluded his supplication, his head instantly shot up when he heard the doorbell. "That's her!" he cried excitedly, his eyes growing as wide as proverbial saucers.

Asher didn't know who was at the door. The only thing he did know was that it *couldn't* be Marnie. For the time being, he ignored it, more concerned with his son's reaction and how to let him down gently. Four was an extremely vulnerable age.

"Jace, I already told you, she went to the movies tonight. Her phone's turned off. By the time she gets this message, you'll be asleep a long time."

"No, I won't," the boy argued. "And that's her at the door!"

Asher didn't know whether just to give in to the boy or try to get him to be reasonable. Neither option sounded all that promising at the moment.

And who the hell was ringing his doorbell at this time of night? he thought impatiently as the chimes went through their refrain again.

It was probably one of his brothers, Asher decided as he crossed to the front door. He was *not* in the friendliest of moods at the moment.

"Yes?" he all but shouted as he yanked open the front door.

It wasn't one of his brothers.

Marnie looked somewhat taken aback by the barked greeting.

"I decided to come over and—and—and put Jace to bed," she finally said, losing her nerve at the last moment. What Nicole had coached her to say was that she had come here to find out if he wanted to finish what he'd started last night.

Confronted with the man and looking up into his face, Marnie felt suddenly unsure of herself. It was a completely novel reaction, one she had never experienced before because ordinarily she felt *quite* confident and self-assured.

Just what kind of an effect was this man having on her?

"You're magical!" Jace joyously exclaimed, throwing his arms around her. Since he was so small, all he managed to do was wrap his arms partway around the lower part of her hips. "Daddy said you were at the movies, but all I had to do was ask you to come over and you did. You're here!"

There was no mistaking the awe in his voice. The

kind of awe that she found really difficult to turn away from or ignore.

"See, Daddy?" Jace craned his neck for a moment, looking at his father as he continued to hold on to Marnie. "I told you she'd come here for me." He turned his attention back to Marnie and told her, "I've got the book all picked out already. I picked it out this morning so it would be ready for you."

Talk about being prepared. But then, Jace had never followed the normal rules that governed the behavior of the average four-year-old. He'd been unique from the moment he was born, Asher thought.

"I do believe you have yourself a budding fan club here in my son," he told Marnie.

"I'm very flattered," Marnie replied, draping her arm around the boy's small shoulders. "Okay, now you scoot upstairs and get ready for bed. I'll be up in a few minutes to tuck you in."

Rather than take her at her word, when she withdrew her arm, Jace was quick to lace his fingers through her hand.

"Come with me, Marnie." He was smart enough to add a heartfelt "Please?" to his entreaty.

"How can I refuse such a charming young man?" she responded. It was clear that she wasn't even going to try. "Okay, let's go upstairs."

As he had the evening before, Asher followed his son and the object of Jace's affection up the stairs to the boy's room.

Once inside, Jace began to hurry out of his regular play clothes and into his pajamas.

It took him all of five minutes to change his clothes, brush his teeth, present Marnie with his selection for that evening's story and then climb into bed, pulling his covers up around himself.

His bright blue eyes were all but riveted to her.

He was ready.

Marnie wasn't about to disappoint him. Picking up the storybook, she got started reading.

To Asher's utter amazement, it took exactly four pages for his son's eyes to close. And two more pages for the boy's breathing to sound even and measured. And peaceful.

Marnie read two more pages after that—slowly— just to be sure the boy was really asleep. Easing the book closed, she watched Jace's small face, all the while alert for any telltale movements to indicate that the boy wasn't really asleep.

But he was, and asleep, Jace looked just like any other four-year-old little boy.

Angelic.

Talk about looks being deceptive, she mused with a smile.

Quietly getting off the rocking chair next to Jace's bed, she placed the storybook on the cushion and tiptoed out of the room.

Asher, she'd noticed, was looking at her differently than he had been yesterday.

Just what was behind that look?

Was he having his doubts?

In reviewing what had occurred last night, would he just rather she just quietly faded off into the sunset instead of being here?

Sorry, she thought. *No can do.*

She'd never been one to cut bait and run—and she'd never been more not inclined to do that than right now. She wanted to see this through to whatever conclusion it might lead to.

No matter what.

Unable to contain himself any longer, Asher turned to look at the woman his son adored, facing her at the bottom of the stairs to ask, "How did you do that?"

She'd stopped abruptly when Asher asked his question. Consequently, she was left standing on the last step.

Marnie wasn't sure just what he was referring to. "How did I do what?"

"Appear on our doorstep like that just as Jace finished begging you to come over on the phone? I thought you told me that you were having dinner and then going to see a movie. With a friend," he added with an emphasis that Marnie thought sounded a little forced and stilted.

"I was," she told him, "but halfway through dinner, there was a sudden change of plans."

She was *not* about to tell him that Nicole had said she needed to find out if that kiss had been just a one-time thing or if they had some sort of a future—however short-lived—together.

"I didn't spoil any of your plans by showing up now, did I?" she asked, suddenly realizing that she'd taken a great deal for granted, coming over like this without giving him any sort of warning.

"No, no plans," he assured her. "But you did just make my evening a whole lot easier by reading to him. He insists that only you have the magic touch." When she looked at him quizzically, he explained, "When I asked him if he thought you read stories better than I did, he gave me an emphatic 'yes.'"

She cringed inwardly for Asher, knowing how she would have felt if her son had told her he preferred having a relative stranger read to him over her.

"Kids are brutally honest at that age," she told him. "They don't realize that other people—especially parents—have feelings, too. Not to mention that they don't always mean what they say."

Jace's comment hadn't really bothered him. He knew what was behind it. The boy missed having a woman in his life.

That, he couldn't help thinking, made two of them.

The only difference was that Jace had no trouble giving his heart away again. It wasn't all that easy for Asher, given that he was still sporting the scars from what had happened the last time he surrendered his heart.

Asher steered the conversation in a slightly different direction. "Well, he certainly has an abundance of feelings, I'll give him that. He's been moping most of the day, asking when you were coming over. He wasn't very happy when I kept telling him that you were busy. You seem to be the highlight of his day."

She smiled. "That's very sweet, but he'll get tired of having me around soon enough," she predicted. She was well aware of how delicate the balance in a relationship between father and son could be at this early stage of development, and she didn't want Asher to feel that he was losing the boy to her.

"Truth be told," Asher continued as if she hadn't just said anything, "you're the highlight of my day, too."

Stunned, Marnie was at a loss how to respond for a moment.

"And," Asher continued, "I have a feeling that neither one of us is going to get tired of having you come around anytime in the foreseeable future."

His words totally took her breath away.

Marnie had expected just the opposite response from him. What she'd expected to hear was his denying that there was anything between them and even a flippant dismissal of the electricity that the kiss they'd shared last night had produced.

She pressed her lips together and finally murmured, "I don't know what to say."

"Don't say anything," he replied. He hadn't told her that because he wanted to discuss the pros and cons with her. It had slipped out because it was the truth. "Just be here a little while longer," he requested.

They were in the living room now, standing toe-to-toe. Close enough for her to feel the heat of his body and she was fairly certain that he could feel the heat from hers.

The very thought stirred her to the point that it was difficult not to just throw her arms around Asher and kiss him.

But that just might push him back, and she definitely didn't want that.

She still hadn't made up her mind if Asher was a man who felt more comfortable doing the pursuing, or if being pursued was just as seductive to him. For her part, she was open to anything, but she had to admit that the thought of being the object of his pursuit was definitely appealing to her.

"I wasn't planning on going anywhere," she told him, her voice barely above a low, seductive and intoxicating whisper.

Asher told himself to take it slow, to stand on a little ceremony. After all, if you've been away from the water for six months and had barely gotten your toes wet in over practically a year, you didn't just immediately dive into the deep end of the pool, not without severe consequences.

Instead, you tested the waters first, gauged its temperature, went slowly...

"Oh, the hell with it," Asher finally muttered under his breath just before he dove in.

"Excuse me?" Marnie said, confused. Or at least that was what she started to say. But the second part of that quickly faded away as her mouth was suddenly laid siege to by his.

He stole her breath away in the very next moment.

Marnie didn't care. This was as close to ecstasy as she felt she was ever going to get, and she intended to enjoy the *hell* out of it before it stopped, or she woke up, whichever came first.

The moment contact was made, Marnie gave herself permission to enjoy what was happening and to also pull out all the stops.

She intended to go as far as she could on this ride, and if it went the full course, well, so be it. If that happened, it would be, she knew, a grand night to remember.

It was, she thought as the kiss between them continued to thrive and deepen, as if her whole body were on fire.

Her pulse accelerating, Marnie deliberately savored every pass of his mouth, every nuance that was involved. With each second that went by, her excitement heightened, along with her desire for more.

The kiss deepened further, opening up a bottomless chasm beneath her.

And then, just as she thought she was going to be forced to tear the clothes right off his body, Asher pulled his head back altogether.

The thought that he was stopping—just like that—brought a cold, foreboding chill along her spine, encompassing all of her and temporarily holding her an unwilling prisoner.

"Am I going too fast?" he asked. "Do you want me to stop?"

She stared at him. Asher Fortune had to be the most selfless man ever created.

But right now she didn't want selfless; she wanted torrid.

"Am I complaining?" she asked in a barely audible, husky whisper.

It wasn't anything she'd said; it was just a feeling he'd had. "No."

"Well, then?" was all Marnie asked before she offered up her mouth to him again.

He needed no more of an invitation than that.

Chapter Twelve

This time, it was Marnie who was the one who abruptly pulled back.

It took Asher a moment to realize that she wasn't just leaning back against the sofa; she was actually pulling away.

It took him another few moments of inner struggle to regain some sort of control over himself, since at this point, all he wanted to do was to be with her, to hold her, to make love with her and just completely lose himself in the essence that was Marnie.

Putting the brakes on—*hard*—really cost him. But although he felt as if his need for Marnie was all but overwhelming, one thing was clear to him. Asher knew he couldn't force himself on her. Couldn't allow this to just be a one-sided exercise aimed to satisfy himself at her expense. The cost was much too high for him morally.

There was no way he could allow that to happen—to either of them.

"I'm sorry," he apologized, the words tumbling awkwardly from his lips as he backed away and rebuttoned the shirt he'd come very close to shedding just now. "I didn't mean to assume—"

He got no further.

Marnie had placed her finger on his lips, stopping the flow of words he was attempting to tender as an apology to her.

"You didn't assume anything wrong," she told him, her voice low and thick with desire. She saw Asher looking at her in total confusion. "But we can't do it here," she went on. "Jace might wake up and come looking for you. Four is just too young to begin this kind of an education."

Marnie was right. How could he have been so irresponsible? Asher upbraided himself.

"I'm an idiot," he declared with a gut-wrenching sigh.

Marnie couldn't suppress the smile that rose to her lips. "You are many things, Asher Fortune. But an idiot isn't one of them." Fastening her own shirt, she left the shirttails hanging out and took his hand. As he looked at her with a silent question in his eyes, she said, "Come. There's just been a change in the venue, not in the activity."

And with that, she headed back toward the staircase and led the way up to the master bedroom.

His room.

Asher would have followed her to the ends of the earth. His bedroom was definitely along the way.

Anticipation went up a little higher within Marnie with each step she took that brought her closer to his bedroom. She'd never shied away from a relationship, but she had never taken this sort of an initiative before. Never led the way, never felt this eager.

But then, she'd never wanted another man the way she found herself wanting Asher. It felt as if rather than helping Asher find his way in life, Asher was the piece of her that had been missing all this time. She'd felt it the moment their hands had touched, the moment he'd kissed her.

Unlike the other men she'd been involved with before, Asher completed her.

It wasn't all just one-sided. He wasn't her project to complete, or a lost soul whom she could help find his way again.

She *needed* him as much as he needed her.

The moment they crossed the threshold into his room and Asher closed the door behind them, the safeguards came down.

All thought of hesitation vanished. Marnie and he were of a single mind, a single thought. To be with each other, to make love with each other while this perfect moment existed, before the world intruded and reality pushed its way in.

He pulled her into his arms, sealing his mouth to hers. The rapid beating of her heart against his chest told him everything he wanted to know.

She was as much in the moment as he was.

He could *feel* his heart echoing hers.

Everything inside him cried, *Hurry! Hurry before something happens to stop this.* But even so, Asher found himself wanting to go slow, to savor the moment.

To savor her.

Still kissing Marnie, he moved from her lips to the slope of her throat. At the same time, he slowly undressed her, removing her clothes the way he might remove wrapping paper from a precious, long-desired, long-anticipated gift.

Savoring the journey as much as he would savor the destination when he reached it.

With each article of clothing that fell away, he could feel his anticipation heightening.

He could feel Marnie's heart keeping time with his own. That, too, excited him, stirring him to head-spinning heights.

Unable to contain herself, Marnie began taking his clothing off, as well, so that when her buttons were undone, so were his. When her shirtsleeves slid off her shoulders, so did his.

The room was warm, but she still felt chills going up her spine.

And when he undid the notch in her belt, undoing the snap and guiding her jeans down her hips in what had to be the most achingly slow movement she'd ever experienced, Marnie made sure that she did the same with the jeans he had on.

When her jeans finally slid down her legs to her ankles and pooled down around her feet to the floor, she stepped out of them.

As did he out of his.

"You've got one more article of clothing on than I do," Asher pointed out when they were both standing there in only their underwear. He lowered his eyes to hers. "No fair," he teased.

It was then that Marnie surprised him by reaching behind her back and releasing the clasp that held her bra in place.

The white lacy demi-bra with its soft blue-ribbon trim seemed to sigh, relaxing its embrace of her breasts. The material slipped away a little, allowing him to get a peek of just enough skin to tantalize him.

The next moment, the bra was gone, a thing of the past.

Asher filled his hands with her. Massaging her breasts in slow, measured strokes, he was slowly making himself completely crazy.

Her moan only increased his sense of urgent need.

The kisses deepened as he tried to fill his soul with her, as well.

Asher caught his breath as he felt the palms of her hands splayed along his naked skin. It took a second for him to realize that she was divesting him of the last piece of material separating him from her.

He followed suit automatically without even stopping

to think about it, removing the blue-and-white scrap of lace serving as her last piece of underwear. He flung it aside, wanting his hands free to be able to be filled with her again.

His mouth sealed to hers, as was his body, they sank down onto his king-size bed.

Needs exploded.

And then Asher got down to business, and Marnie discovered what true ecstasy really was.

She could feel them, could feel the incredible tiny bursts of energy erupting at her very core with each pass of his clever fingers, each languid swipe of his lingering lips and tongue.

Especially his tongue.

As she arched, shifted and bucked, too filled with pure, unadulterated pleasure to stand it, she was also determined not to allow it to end. She came to the edge of sanity, relishing every fantastic nuance, every quiver of her body in response to his.

Grabbing his shoulders after a particularly wildly incredible experience, she panted out his name as she tried to feebly drag Asher back up to her level.

"You don't do it now," she whispered in a raspy, gravelly voice, "and there won't be anything left of me and then I won't be able, however inadequately, to return this favor."

One final thrust of his tongue to send her tumbling over the edge and then he raised himself up on his hands, slowly dragging his body up along hers, setting her on fire all over again. As for him, the match was already lit and the flame was beginning to work its way up to the end of the wick.

"Ready or not," he whispered against her ear, "here I come."

"I'm ready," she managed to get out between gritted teeth. "Oh, so very ready," she assured him eagerly. Her whole body was tingling in fevered anticipation.

Parting her legs for him, Marnie caught her breath as he came to her.

The sound of sheer pleasure escaped her lips as she felt Asher take her, make her his own.

The sense of urgency that came over her was breathtaking. Marnie couldn't seem to shake the feeling that if she didn't hurry, if she didn't urge him to do the same, this would swiftly become a heartbreakingly lost opportunity.

She knew she was being silly, that a wheelbarrow of premonitions didn't amount to a hill of anything, but she moved quickly, as if the very forces of hell were chasing them.

The woman moved to an amazing tempo, Asher couldn't help thinking, and he actually had to be quick in order to match it. Not about to be left behind, he moved his hips as quickly as she did, increasing the tempo right along with her and even moving slightly ahead until it was hard to say who was outracing whom.

He wanted to cry out her name, to shout it out to the world, but he knew that he couldn't, so he struggled to remain as silent as possible.

But a moan did escape. Whether it was hers or his,

he couldn't have said for sure. All he knew was that the wave of pleasure that washed over him was like none he'd ever felt before.

It even took him a moment to realize that he was holding her so tightly he was in danger of squeezing her past the limit of endurance.

The last thing he wanted was to end this episode by hurting her.

He released Marnie, albeit reluctantly. Holding her to him like this felt as if he were sealing her into his heart.

Asher didn't want to attempt to explore what that really meant to him right now, or why he had even thought of it. He only knew that this was something exquisitely different, exquisitely new, and he felt both humbled and overwhelmed in its presence.

Even so, he was gun-shy, which meant that he was a little leery of anything his feelings declared right now. After all, it was his feelings that had pushed him into marrying Lynn in the first place.

Bad call there, he couldn't help thinking.

The descent from the peak they had reached together was far too swift to please him.

He drew in a long breath, and then another, attempting to regulate both his breathing and his heart. Neither was being very cooperative.

Asher turned his face toward hers, not really knowing what to say, how to acknowledge what had just happened. What did you say to a woman who had rocked your world?

No single word or group of words that came to mind seemed nearly adequate.

He began with the most responsible thing he could say, getting it out of the way first. "I didn't hurt you, did I?"

Dazed, still floating on a euphoric cloud of pink cotton candy, Marnie murmured, "Hmm?" to what she presumed was a question.

Asher drew himself up on his elbow so that he could get a better view of her face. Right now it was all but buried in the shadows.

"I didn't hurt you, did I?" he asked again, this time with a tad more concern in his voice.

Rather than answer outright, she turned into him and smiled up into his eyes.

Deeply.

She was still somewhat dazed and oh-so-reluctant to disembark from the wild, interplanetary ride she'd just been on.

"No," she finally managed to say. "Why would you think you hurt me?" she had to ask.

"I was afraid I got too carried away, too physical," he confessed.

Her words were still emerging from her lips in slow motion. "And that's a bad thing?"

"Not for me," he allowed, but as far as he was concerned, he wasn't the one who counted here. "I was thinking about you—"

"Not for me, either," she breathed, punctuating each

breathy word with a smile that progressively widened with each syllable.

When she looked at him like that, all he could think of was doing it again, despite the fact that he felt weak enough to allow an undernourished cat with a limp to wipe the floor with him.

"You're sure?" he pressed.

"Very sure," she answered solemnly. And then, summoning whatever latent strength she had stored up for just such an emergency, Marnie drew herself up, turned and suddenly, he was the one beneath her and she was the one on top. "As a matter of fact, let me show you just how sure of that I am," she offered.

Before he could say a single word, either in protest or to urge her on, Marnie splayed her body over his and sealed her mouth to his lips.

This time, the moan of pleasure that echoed between them belonged to him.

He felt her smile widening over his lips, could have sworn he heard a triumphant laugh emerge from her and find its way into him.

It was, just as before, all the invitation that he needed. He could feel himself filling with anticipation, wanting her as if he hadn't just had her minutes ago.

Nothing else mattered but this moment, this woman and the rising heat between them.

He took her all over again.

And savored it as if it were the first time.

Chapter Thirteen

"Daddy!"

The urgent, distressed cry scissored through the contented drowsiness that had crept over Marnie and had, against her innate common sense, caused her to remain in Asher's bed.

Right beside Asher.

Intense lovemaking, not once but twice that evening, had left her—she suspected that it had left *both* of them—really exhausted. It was a very nice, comfortable exhaustion, the kind that caused a person to slip into sleep with a very broad, immensely contented smile.

But the sudden desperate cry coming from the bedroom down the hall had abruptly and quickly changed the atmosphere, ushering in reality and reminding Marnie that she wasn't supposed to be staying the night—or any part of the night, for that matter. Her plan had been to leave after her heartbeat had ceased crashing wildly.

Somewhere along the line, that plan had gotten lost and been forgotten.

And they had both fallen asleep.

But they were both awake now.

Clutching the blanket and sheet up against her torso, Marnie bolted upright, instantly placing the source of the noise.

"Jace," she cried, concerned.

The next moment, Asher, utterly alert now, was sitting up, as well.

But not beside her.

Marnie had already bounded out of bed and was searching for her own clothes through the strewn, miscellaneous articles of clothing on the floor. Finding them, she was hurrying into her underwear, jeans and shirt as fast as humanly possible.

She was half dressed before Asher's bare feet hit the floor.

"It's probably a nightmare," Asher told her. "He has them sometimes. Not as often as he used to now that he's grown attached to you," he added as he pulled up his jeans. In a hurry, he'd deliberately skipped putting on his underwear.

She tried very hard not to focus on the fact that all there was between Asher and his exceedingly sculpted, hard naked body was just a length of denim. This was no time to start drooling, she ordered herself sharply—

but who knew that a former financial VP turned rancher could have a body that brought the word *Adonis* to mind?

"You need to go to him," she prompted.

"You're leaving?" Asher asked, reading between the lines as he watched her get dressed. Disappointment as well as an unexpected flash of guilt, encroached over him in annoying waves.

"Dad-deee!"

She nodded in response to his question. There was no other choice open to her, and they both knew it.

"The last thing Jace needs is to find me in Daddy's bed. Now go, go!" she urged, waving him to the other room as she pulled her boots on.

Asher lingered for a second in the doorway. He wanted her to know. "I don't want you to go," he told her honestly.

Ambivalent feelings be damned, he thought. He *wanted* her in his bed.

She found his protest immensely endearing and more touching than she had thought possible. There weren't enough words available to tell him, so she merely quietly said, "I know." Dressed, she got up behind him and pushed Asher across the threshold, into the hall. "Now go, he needs you, and Jace comes first, before everything."

He knew that. He'd always felt that way, too. But faced with the reality of it, he couldn't help feeling a desire to hold on to Marnie, as well.

Prior to tonight, he hadn't thought that he even *wanted* to be with another woman. And he really hadn't felt up to facing and tackling all the hoops that required his jumping through them when it came to maintaining a relationship.

But Marnie made it easy.

Maybe *too* easy.

He hesitated one last time, at the mercy of dueling emotions. "Sure you don't want to stay?"

Thinking that she could stay would only wind up torturing her. In her heart, she knew that staying wasn't the right thing to do.

Marnie shook her head. "Jace is a very bright boy. Seeing me here like this will raise too many questions. Questions I don't think you really want to answer yet."

She suspected that Jace would think they were a couple and say as much to his father. Hearing Asher deny it—as she expected he would—was something *she* wasn't up to facing right now.

Still, she saw Asher hesitating even as his son cried out for him a third time, his small voice swelling to grand proportions and filling up every tiny space of the night air.

"You'll come back tomorrow?" Asher asked.

She nodded. "I'll come back tomorrow." *Wild horses couldn't keep me away.* "Now go to him," she urged again, "before Jace thinks the whole house was abducted by aliens."

With a nod, Asher began to go, then stopped and spun around to look at her one final time. Impulsively, he hurried back and brushed his lips against hers before retreating down the hall.

Marnie stood where she was for a long moment, watching him disappear into Jace's room. She passed her fingertips lightly along her lips.

She could still feel the imprint of his last kiss.

Her rapid pulse rate started up all over again.

She knew she should be going *now,* before Jace could accidentally see her out here like this. But just for a second, love—and curiosity—got the better of her.

Taking a few steps toward Jace's room, she stopped just short of the door and listened as Asher did his best to quiet Jace's sobs.

As he entered his son's bedroom, Asher flipped on the light-switch dimmer only halfway. Just enough to chase away whatever specters Jace might have imagined were there in his room.

He knew how that could be. He could remember growing up with the same sort of fears.

Asher had gotten a night-light for the boy, and it was always on from the moment he went to bed, but this was the kind of nightmare that required something stronger than the tiny illumination that came from the single five-watt bulb.

The light had to chase away something more than just dim shadows.

"Hey, buddy, what's going on?" he asked as if he were stopping by the room just to shoot the breeze with his son. Asher sat down near the head of Jace's bed.

Jace instantly scrambled up so that he could get close to him and huddled in his arms. Only after he'd settled in and felt as if he was protected did the boy finally blurt out what was bothering him.

"A bad man came," Jace cried.

Holding the boy to him, Asher stroked the silky blond hair, hoping the contact would soothe Jace enough to calm him down.

"It was just a nightmare, son. There's no bad man here," he assured him in a low, tranquil voice. "There's just you and me here, nobody else." Even as he said it, he ached a little, thinking of Marnie.

Jace raised his tear-streaked face, looking up at his father. "No, he *took* her, Daddy," he insisted again, trying to make him understand. "The bad man took Mommy away with him."

Out of the mouths of babes, Asher couldn't help thinking, remembering that one of his brothers had told him Lynn was engaged again. This after she'd told him that she just wasn't ready for marriage and *really* wasn't ready for motherhood.

Apparently what she'd meant at the time was that she wasn't ready to be married to *him,* and really wasn't ready to parent *his* child, which was the way he knew she thought of Jace. Not as *theirs* but as *his.*

The discovery of her engagement still smarted and had delivered a pretty crushing blow to his ego. But he was working his way through that and he was getting better all the time.

But having Jace talk about Lynn, even though a nightmare was responsible for bringing her up, reminded him once again that as a judge of character, he made a great rancher.

And that in turn made him wonder—what if he was wrong about Marnie, as well?

Struggling, Asher banked down the fresh wave of hurt that threatened to seize him. He wasn't completely successful, but he continued working at it.

Out loud, he told his son, "A bad man didn't take Mommy away, Jace. She just didn't want to be with me anymore. Not you," he said quickly, knowing how Jace's mind worked. He was determined to spare the boy's feelings as much as possible. "If she could have taken you with her, she would have, but I wouldn't let her."

It was a lie—she hadn't wanted to take Jace with her—and it made him uncomfortable to lie to his son, but at the same time, he felt that in this case, it was necessary.

"I wanted you so much, I was afraid that my heart would break if she took you away with her."

Jace was hanging on every word. For now, the night-mare he'd just had was temporarily forgotten. "I won't let your heart break, Daddy," he promised.

"Good boy," Asher said, patting the boy's shoulder. Thinking the crisis over, he got up and started to cross to the doorway. "Well, good night, son."

"Daddy?" Jace called out uncertainly.

So near and yet so far, Asher couldn't help thinking, turning around again.

He supposed that it was ultimately a good thing that Marnie had left. He wouldn't have wanted her waiting indefinitely for his return and apparently, he wasn't going anywhere just yet.

"Yes?"

He saw Jace's eyes sweep fearfully around his room, looking especially hard into corners. "The bad man might come back."

"The bad man won't come back," Asher tried to assure him.

He wasn't convincing enough.

"But he might," Jace insisted. The next moment, he gave his father the solution. "Can I stay with you tonight?"

Lynn would have berated him for being too permissive. But then, Lynn wasn't exactly up for a parent-of-the-year award, now, was she? he asked himself. So rather than stand there and tell his four-year-old son that he needed to "man up," the way he knew that Lynn—and his own father, for that matter, another person not up for that award this year, or any other year, either—would say, he held his hand out toward the boy in a show of support.

"C'mon, let's get back to my room before dawn finds us."

Jace scrambled out of bed and came to his side faster than Asher would have thought possible. The boy snuggled up against him much in the same way a pet puppy might to show affection.

Raising this little boy was a huge responsibility. He only hoped he was up to it and did right by him.

Asher felt a definite pang as he entered his room with his son.

It was empty.

He supposed a part of him—a very small part of him, he silently insisted—had hoped to find Marnie there even though he knew she was right about leaving.

The fact that he automatically looked for her worried him.

Jace quickly scooted into the king-size bed ahead of him, automatically taking the right side because he knew his father preferred the left.

As Asher began to get in on his side, Jace suddenly exclaimed, "Marnie!"

Asher had to stop himself from looking around—she wouldn't still be here, would she?

Holding his breath a moment in an effort to regulate his heartbeat so that it was back to normal, Asher told him, "Marnie went home a long time ago, Jace."

It was all relative, he thought, absolving himself of the white lie. Lengths of time increased when you were younger.

He saw Jace's small brows knit themselves together closely, giving him the appearance of someone contemplating an extremely large puzzle.

"The bed smells like Marnie," he told his father. As if to prove his point—and verify his findings—Jace stuck his face down into the sheet and blanket on his side and took in a deep, exaggerated breath.

Clearly finding evidence to support his declaration,

he looked up again, his blue eyes darting toward his father.

"How come the sheet and blanket smell like Marnie?" he wanted to know.

Asher's mind raced around madly, searching for something plausible to offer in the way of an explanation. He told the boy the only thing that had come to mind.

"I guess she must have been up here and changed the bedding. She said that everyone should sleep on fresh linens," he added, recalling something that Marnie actually *had* said. "Sheets," he explained when Jace's face began to pucker in consternation all over again.

"Oh," Jace said, nodding and seemingly accepting the explanation his father had tendered.

Asher began to settle back against his pillows—Marnie had obviously neatened all this just before she left. He congratulated himself on being so "quick on his feet" and coming up with what Jace deemed to be an acceptable answer.

The next moment, the boy turned toward him in the bed. Asher could see by the look on Jace's face that he wasn't out of the woods yet.

Sure enough, a couple of seconds later, Jace asked, "How come she didn't change my sheets?"

"Good question," Asher agreed. "I guess I'm going to have to ask her why she forgot to change yours." He was stalling for time, but another excuse didn't present itself.

Jace had a possible solution for him. "Maybe she ran out of time," he said to his father.

Asher was more than happy to grasp on to anything as long as it made the boy stop asking questions. "Maybe," he answered, nodding again in agreement. "Now, why don't you—"

"Daddy?" Jace interjected before he could tell him to go to sleep.

Now what? Asher wondered impatiently, then forced himself to push his impatience aside. The kid, he decided, was going to have a great legal mind someday. He was willing to bet money on that.

"Yes, Jace?"

"Don't ask Marnie why she didn't change my sheets," he requested.

While he would have wanted to believe that this was finally the end of this drawn-out discussion, Asher's curiosity had been piqued and he couldn't help asking, "Why not?"

Jace had a very good reason for his request. He'd thought it all out, leaving nothing to chance. Convinced that he had to help his father before Marnie walked out on them, too.

"Because she might think you were telling her that she forgot to do something and I don't want her to get mad and go away," the boy told him honestly. "I don't care about the sheets," he said with feeling. "I just want Marnie coming back to us."

If she came back each day because of Jace, Asher thought, then they could keep on seeing each other, leaving everything just the way it was.

He liked that.

"Sounds good to me," Asher agreed.

"I like Marnie," the boy added needlessly. His eyes beginning to close, he asked, "How about you, Daddy? Do you like her?"

He knew Jace would keep after him until he got the answer he wanted to hear. Agreeing at the outset just saved him some time, Asher reasoned.

"Yes, I like her," he answered.

But apparently Jace wasn't through. "A lot?" he wanted to know.

Asher knew he was in too deep to reverse course now, so he said, "Yes, a lot."

"Good," Jace responded, a long, relieved breath punctuating the single word.

It was the last thing Jace said before finally falling asleep.

The same answer that had allowed Jace to fall asleep was the one that was destined to keep Asher awake for several more hours to come before he could finally reach the same state as his son.

Chapter Fourteen

He was moving too fast.

Asher knew he had to put on the brakes. He just had to assure himself that what he felt for Marnie was not a lasting emotion.

He was rushing through the stages of a relationship in order to arrive at what might have been an inevitable reaction, a reaction that hadn't been given enough time to develop at an acceptable pace.

People on the rebound did that.

There was no other conclusion for Asher to reach, early the next day, but that he had to be on the rebound from his failed marriage. And he didn't have to be told what happened to relationships that were formed because one of the participants was on the rebound.

He knew.

They were doomed to failure.

He'd had enough of failure.

What he was doing was trying to fill the void, the emptiness he felt inside him. He'd freely admitted to himself that he wanted to love again, to *be* in love again, and maybe that need was what was coloring the way he looked at Marnie.

In his desire to blot out what had transpired in his life not all that long ago, was he on the verge of making another huge mistake? A man in his state certainly wasn't clearheaded enough to make lasting decisions, that much he was aware of.

The truth of it was that the very sight of Marnie stirred him to such a point that making rational decisions seemed to be completely out of his realm.

What if he actually married Marnie and then it turned out that they were all wrong for each other? He couldn't put Jace through another divorce. Couldn't put *himself* through another divorce.

Better to back off and just take this at a slow, responsible pace.

Better yet, he thought in the next moment, he should call for a time-out. That way, he could see if, separated from Marnie, he wound up missing her more with each passing day.

Or if, as the days went on, his feelings for her progressively lessened. It would be a way of discovering if, in his case, it was a matter of absence making the heart grow fonder.

If it was the latter, then he'd know for certain that what

he was feeling right now was all due to his being on the rebound.

And if it turned out to be the former, then for once, he'd really lucked out.

But there was only one thing wrong with his going forward with his little experiment. He needed Marnie to watch his son, and he knew that Jace would be utterly devastated, not to mention completely unmanageable, if she suddenly dropped out of his life. For better or worse, the boy was attached to her.

Almost as attached as he was, Asher couldn't help thinking.

Again, he really needed to know if what he was feeling was genuine or just something he'd created because of his intense desire to be part of a unit. Was he attracted to Marnie because of Marnie, or because he couldn't deal with the loneliness that was echoing inside him?

When she was around, he tended to think that what he was experiencing was very, very real. It was only when she was out of his sight that he was plagued with these doubts.

Doubts that arose out of the ashes of his failed marriage.

Well, since he couldn't just pick up and call a moratorium on her coming over—not without major repercussions—he would do the next best thing. He would keep his distance until he was sure that what he was feeling was real. He owed it to all three of them.

Marnie noticed the difference in Asher's behavior toward her almost immediately when she arrived later that afternoon.

Anticipating seeing Asher again after the fabulous evening they'd spent discovering each other's bodies, she was stunned when she walked into the house and Asher barely returned her greeting. Hers had been enthusiastic and sunny. His, when he finally responded, was monotone and barely audible.

"Is anything wrong?" she asked.

She found herself saying the words to Asher's back because after opening the front door and muttering the all but inaudible greeting, he'd just turned away from her. He was making his way out of the foyer, even as Jace appeared, grabbed her hand and began tugging her in the direction of the family room.

When Asher gave no indication that he intended to answer her question, or that he had even *heard* her question, she raised her voice and this time used his name to get his attention.

"Is anything wrong, Asher?"

Being aloof was really killing him, but he knew that he *had* to put some distance between them emotionally. Pausing for a second, he spared her a glance over his shoulder. "No, nothing's wrong. What makes you ask?"

He sounded so cold she could only stare at him, stunned.

Had she gotten the wrong signals after all? Had last night been some aberration that she had brought on because she'd been so willing to make love with him? Was this going to be a case of her being nothing more than a notch on his belt?

No! Damn it, she refused to believe that. Asher

wasn't some empty-headed egotistical playboy out for a good time. He'd been tender and sensitive last night. He was a good father, a good man.

Something had to be wrong, and she intended to find out what that something was, even if broaching the subject made her feel somewhat awkward and uncomfortable.

But because Jace was right there, she couldn't ask Asher outright the way she really wanted to, awkward or not.

"No reason," she finally replied quietly.

Maybe this was just a mood and he'd work his way out of it, she thought hopefully. If that *was* the case, then he needed a little space and she could certainly give him that.

Turning to Jace, she smiled at the bright, eager face turned up to hers and asked, "So, what've you got planned for us today?"

It was absolutely the right thing to say because Jace laughed gleefully and declared, "C'mon, you gotta come with me."

At least one of the Fortune men was happy to have her here, she thought ruefully.

Because she couldn't do anything about the situation with Asher right now, she forced herself to put it out of her mind and focused exclusively on the little boy.

After all, that was what she was being paid for.

If she didn't know any better, she thought a couple of days later, she would have said that Asher was deliberately avoiding her. The moment she would put Jace to bed for the night, reading to the boy until he finally fell asleep, Asher seemed to all but disappear into his den, working on something on his computer.

When she tried to ask him about it, Asher told her that he couldn't discuss the matter as it was a confidential project for his family business, JMF Financial.

Hearing him utter those words *really* made her feel like an outsider.

His ongoing—and sudden—coldness ate away at her. *Why* was he doing this? Why was he suddenly behaving this way?

Could he actually be afraid that she was going to try to drag him to the altar? Or blackmail him for some reason? Try to take his money?

Both notions seemed absurd.

There was no doubt in her mind that she was reaching the end of her rope. Every time she tried to talk to Asher about his complete about-face ever since they'd made love, he found some excuse to throw in her path. He'd tell her that he couldn't talk to her now because he was working on a project, or had to make a call, or any one of a number of other flimsy excuses that, from where she was standing, just seemed like another lie.

Why would he lie to her when he *knew* she was completely willing to believe anything he said to her? *She* certainly wouldn't lie to him.

Marnie just did *not* understand what was going on here.

After suffering a great many rebuffs, she just backed

away, trying to safeguard her feelings from another assault—intentional or accidental.

And, after trying in vain to pin Asher down and find out what had brought about this sudden change in him, she made up her mind that two people could play this stupid game. She was not about to give him the satisfaction of seeing just how hurt and disappointed she was with the way he was treating her.

Her pride wouldn't allow it.

Though she'd marched up to his den and stood before his closed door, she turned on her heel and went straight to the front door. Too angry to speak, she was going to go home. And she did, slamming the door in her wake.

Asher heard the front door slam. The sound reverberated through every bone in his body.

She'd left, he thought. Gone home angry. Damn it, he was being stupid, wasting time like this trying to figure out if he was right or wrong in the way he was reacting to her.

For two cents, he would throw up his hands, go back to the way things were and the hell with all the consequences.

Having made up his mind—at least for the moment—Asher was filled with a need to explain to her why he'd been acting like such an idiot. Then he'd beg her to give him another chance to start all over again.

Well, maybe not *all* over again, he amended, but at least do over this last week.

He was all set to go running after her, confident that

she hadn't pulled out of his driveway yet because he hadn't heard her start up her car, when his cell phone rang.

Habit had him pulling his phone out and glancing at the caller ID, thinking—unclearly, granted—that it might be Marnie calling to give him a piece of her mind. He'd listen, then ask for forgiveness.

But the name on the screen belonged to Shane, not the woman who had just slammed his front door. Shane had gone on a fact-hunting trip back to Atlanta. Like it or not, Asher needed to take this.

Feeling incredibly frustrated, not to mention torn, he hit Accept on his phone and bit off a terse "Hello." In the background, he heard Marnie's car starting up. Making a last-ditch attempt, he got to the front door and pulled it open.

She had already backed out of his driveway. He was just in time to see her speeding away.

His heart sank.

"Well, don't *you* sound cheerful?" he heard his brother say on the other end of the call.

Asher didn't bother suppressing his sigh as he closed the door again. He walked back to his den slowly.

Maybe this was for the best after all, he tried to tell himself. He still hadn't come to any real concrete conclusions about what seemed like his feverish actions, and being around Marnie *without* having Jace as a buffer might be a really big mistake on his part.

Again.

"Sorry," he said to Shane. "It's been kind of a rough week."

He heard Shane laugh dryly. "Yeah, tell me about it."

With effort, Asher blocked out all thoughts of Marnie for the moment and shifted his attention to his brother's call. Shane had gone back to Atlanta to try to find out if there was any information to be gathered about the mystery woman in their normally straitlaced father's life, one Jeanne Marie. She was the woman their father had graced with all those shares in the company.

Asher replayed his brother's droll comment in his head. "I don't think we're talking about the same thing," Asher told him.

"Probably not," his brother allowed. "Seeing as how you're in Texas and I'm stuck back here in Atlanta, hitting my head against one dead end after another."

Not exactly the news the rest of them had been waiting for here. "I take it from your cryptic description that you're calling to tell me that there's nothing to tell me."

Again a disparaging laugh prefaced Shane's response. "Yeah, something like that. Dad's lady friend *did* live here in Atlanta, but she's not here anymore. At least *I* can't find her. I went to the address that I found on Dad's personal computer, but she's long gone."

Why should the woman stay in Atlanta when she could travel anywhere on their dime? "She probably decided that she can afford to live high on the hog now that she has all this money."

"Yeah, thanks to the fact that she now has a sugar daddy." Shane groaned at his own description. "Fine, upstanding James Marshall Fortune."

Asher could almost hear his brother shiver. Admittedly, it wasn't the way *anyone* first pictured their austere father. But then, they'd all thought of him as the faithful, loving husband and obviously that hadn't been true, either.

"I'd rather not have that image in my head if it's all the same to you," Asher told his brother.

"Hey, I'm with you, Ash," Shane agreed. "Doesn't change the fact that that's probably what he is to her, though. One piece of news," he continued. "I managed to locate a picture of this Jeanne Marie. Not bad looking, really."

Asher responded by asking the obvious. "Why would he make a homely woman his mistress?"

But to his surprise, rather than go along with his assumption, Shane put the brakes on that line of thinking. "You're jumping to conclusions, Ash. We don't know that this woman *is* his mistress."

What else could the woman be, getting that sort of a "gift" from their father? They knew the man's character well enough to be convinced that the patriarch wouldn't stand for blackmail.

"Well, she sure as hell isn't his adoptive mother," Asher cracked. "Not at her age."

"True," Shane agreed. Asher did have a point. Still, thinking of the woman as their father's mistress really didn't sit well with him. A mistress usually meant that this was a long-term relationship, and he couldn't get himself to believe that the man had been deceiving them all this time, leading a dual life.

"So," Asher asked when Shane had stopped talking for a moment, "what are you going to do now?"

"I thought I'd stay here a couple more days, poke around some more, see if I can't find someone who knows where she went. Maybe I can find a friend of a friend, that sort of thing." There was a trace of impatience in the smooth Southern drawl. "There's got to be some kind of a trail," Shane insisted. "The woman couldn't have just taken those shares and disappeared off the face of the earth."

Despite the sophisticated tracking methods that abounded these days, there were *still* ways a person could fall off the grid if she knew the right people. Maybe Asher and his brothers needed to avail themselves of those kinds of people, he thought.

"Granted," he said to Shane, "but maybe we need to get professional help. You know, like a private investigator."

"Yeah, I thought of that, too," Shane confessed. "I'll let you and the others know what I decide to do after I've figured it out." His tone changed slightly as he asked, "Say, how are you doing?"

"What do you mean?" Asher asked evasively.

Shane would have thought that was self-evident, but he spelled it out for Asher. "Well, in getting settled in Red Rock—and getting on with your life," he added with definite emphasis. Shane had never really cared for his ex-sister-in-law.

"I'm okay."

Asher's tone was far from convincing, Shane thought. "You don't sound okay."

He wasn't, but this was just too complicated to sum up in twenty-five words or fewer across approximately a thousand miles. Asher could feel his patience swiftly unraveling, and he didn't really want to snap at his brother.

"Shane, I already have a mother. I don't need another one."

"Testy," Shane noted dryly. "Does that mean you're finally ready to put that woman behind you—or is something else going on?" he asked suspiciously.

For a second, Asher almost gave in. He was *this close* to telling his brother about the conflicted feelings he was having.

But then, in the next moment, he decided against it. After all, he was a grown man and that meant he was supposed to sort things out for himself, not go running to his brothers and bend their collective ears about his messed-up love life every time there was a new problem to deal with.

"Nothing else," he answered. "And when there is, I'll let you know," he added with finality to forestall any further questions.

Shane wasn't taken in for a moment. But he also wasn't about to pressure his brother for information. "Fine, you do that," he said. "You know where to find me."

Shane wasn't very convincing, Asher thought. Even a child would know that. Any second now, the inquisition was going to begin in earnest. He needed to stop that in its tracks.

"I've got to go," he told Shane, then added the first thing that came to his mind as an excuse. "Jace is calling me."

"You let him stay up so late?" Shane asked in surprise.

"'Let' has nothing to do with it," Asher replied, and then he hung up before Shane could say anything further. He really didn't want to get embroiled in an argument and that was where this exchange between them looked as though it was heading.

The fact that Shane only pressed him because he cared didn't make it any easier to take, Asher thought.

Chapter Fifteen

She just couldn't take it any longer.

Marnie felt as if her heart were being ripped out of her chest one tiny, jagged piece at a time. She'd been turning up at Asher's house every afternoon, promptly after her riding sessions were over, for over a week now and she couldn't take it any longer.

Couldn't take the charade that was going on.

Pretending that she didn't care about Asher, that she wasn't really hurt by his abrupt about-face, was killing her. She had given him every opportunity to apologize, every opportunity to come around, or at least explain why he was acting this way.

Rather than explain, Asher was growing even *more* distant toward her, something she hadn't thought was possible. But it obviously was.

Maybe this was actually the *real* Asher and the other one had been an act. One that he had gotten plainly tired of.

If that *was* the case, then she was lucky she found out now, before she was too heavily invested in the man's life.

Ha, a small voice in her head mocked her. *As if you weren't already* really *involved with this guy.*

Okay, so maybe she was, but she could still take matters into her own hands, still pull back and save herself.

The moment she decided on her course of action, Marnie didn't feel liberated, didn't feel triumphant as she'd hoped she would. What she felt, pure and simple, was guilty. Because she knew that if she stopped coming over, Jace would think he was being abandoned again.

But there was nothing she could do about that. She had to think about herself for once in her life. Right now she was living in a state of limbo, and the only way she was going to be able to move on was to excise Asher and everything that went with him from her life.

That meant cutting ties with Jace, too.

It was a matter of survival.

All the same, she dreaded making the phone call, even though she had her excuse rehearsed and in place. But, dreading it or not, she had to do it. She couldn't very well *not* call and then not turn up. That would leave Asher in a lurch, wondering why she hadn't shown up as per their agreement.

It would have served him right if she didn't call, but

he wasn't the one she was concerned about. She didn't want to leave Jace hanging.

Besides, just because Asher was behaving like a grade-A jerk didn't mean she had to do the same. She was better than that.

Squaring her shoulders, Marnie picked up the landline extension, pulled it onto her lap and dialed Asher's number.

The phone on the other end rang once, then twice, then a third time. She caught herself crossing her fingers that it would ring one more time because then that meant she'd get voice mail. She would really prefer leaving a message to having to talk to Asher in person.

As if in answer to her prayer, she heard the voice mail pick up. The next voice she heard was Asher's.

"You've reached the home of Asher and Jace Fortune. We can't come to the phone right now, but if you leave your name and number, we'll get back to you as soon as we're able."

"Yeah, able." That was Jace in the background, chiming in, she thought fondly.

Taking a breath, she said, "This is Marnie. Something's come up and I'm afraid I won't be able to babysit Jace anymore. Sorry," she added. The word, she couldn't help thinking, didn't begin to cover how she actually felt—not that he cared, she thought ruefully. "Tell Jace goodbye for me. I'll miss him," she added deliberately.

Asher, she thought angrily, was probably too thick to pick up her message.

And then she hung up—quickly before the sob she felt welling up in her throat came out and betrayed her.

"What came up?"

Marnie nearly jumped out of her skin. Whirling around in her seat, she saw that her mother was standing directly behind the sofa she was sitting on. Gloria McCafferty looked rather perplexed.

"I know that those heart-to-heart talks we used to have occurred strictly because you were still a preteen and now that you're all grown up I don't expect for you to tell me *everything*," her mother tactfully emphasized as she came around to join her on the sofa. "But I did think that you'd give me a summarized update of what was going on in your life—the PG-rated stuff—at least every once in a while."

There was both sympathy and a faint look of expectation in Gloria's eyes as she sat down and placed her hand over her daughter's. She was every inch the classic mother, her own heart aching whenever she sensed that her child's did.

"What came up?" she asked again, trying to coax the information out of Marnie.

Marnie sighed and shook her head. "Nothing, Mom. Really."

Instead of clearing anything up, that only brought up more questions. "Then why did you—?"

She really, really didn't want to talk about it. It hurt too much. "Look, I thought you above all people would be glad I decided not to work for Asher Fortune anymore. After all, you were the one who said you didn't want me taking in any more 'strays,' remember?" Marnie reminded her mother tersely.

"And I still don't," Gloria told her. Unable to help herself, she pushed the hair out of her daughter's face. "Because I worry about you getting hurt."

Marnie lifted her chin defensively. "Well, I can't get hurt if I'm not there, can I?"

Gloria took that same chin in her hand and looked at her daughter's face closely. She saw all she needed to know there.

"You already *are* hurt, aren't you, honey?"

It drove Marnie crazy that her mother could just delve into her head like that and read her like a book. She thought of voicing a denial, contradicting her mother's assumption, but something in the pit of her stomach told her that it was futile.

"Doesn't matter," she murmured with a vague shrug.

"It matters to me," Gloria insisted. "I wasn't telling you not to get involved, Marnie. I *want* you to be involved. I want you to have someone in your life, a good man who'll love you and see you for the rare person you are. I want you to have a family with this man. I was just warning you to be careful because I know what a huge heart you have. There are some men out there who would use that strictly for their advantage. I just didn't want you becoming a victim."

"Well, you can put your worries to rest, Mom. I'm just going to be teaching kids how to ride at the stables for a while. No more babysitting." She knew she couldn't bear it. It would just remind her of Asher and Jace.

"What happened, Marnie?" her mother asked gently.

Because she desperately needed to unload to someone, at least a tiny bit, Marnie gave her mother an abbreviated, bare-bones summary of the problem. Since she didn't want to go into any details, what she did was simply say, "He wasn't interested."

Her answer left Gloria utterly speechless for a moment. Recovering, she said, "Well, just as well, then. You wouldn't want to get involved with a stupid man, now, would you?"

Without thinking, Marnie was instantly defensive of the man who'd taken her heart prisoner so callously. "He's not stupid."

"Oh, but I beg to differ. Anyone who wouldn't be interested in a young woman as beautiful, as intelligent and as hardworking as you are *has* to be stupid. He might deserve your pity, but he definitely deserves nothing else." She offered her daughter an encouraging smile. "I'd say you dodged a bullet there, Marnie."

I don't feel like I dodged a bullet, Mom. I feel like it hit me right in the heart.

Marnie rolled her eyes in response to her mother's words. "Mother, you're prejudiced."

"Possibly," Gloria allowed generously. "But I also have eyes. That in turn allows me to recognize both your faults—your heart's way too big—and your virtues, which are too numerous for me to mention at this time," she deadpanned.

"Oh? Why?" Marnie asked innocently. She had never

known her mother to pass up an opportunity to talk, especially at length.

"Because if I do—" Gloria rose to her feet "—I'll make you late for your eager little students." As her daughter stood up as well, Gloria patted her on the shoulder, a gesture of comfort as well as one of pride. "They just might go riding off on their own, and you'd have to spend half the afternoon looking for them."

The scenario her mother had verbally drawn was intentionally melodramatic. Picturing it, Marnie couldn't help laughing.

"Thanks, Mom, I needed that," she told her. It really did feel good to laugh.

"Just doing my job, dear," she assured Marnie. "I'm your mother. I'm supposed to be able to cheer you up." She kissed Marnie's forehead. "Now go teach. Be with people who appreciate you."

Marnie started to cross the living room, intent on picking up her purse and car keys so that she could be on her way. "I love you, Mom."

"And I, you," Gloria responded. They both knew that was a given.

"But *why* can't Marnie come over?" Jace whined, asking the question for what had to be the thousandth time since Asher had told his son the upshot of the message she'd left on his voice mail several days ago.

It had been five days since he'd heard that message. Five days and he hadn't been able to get her on the phone so they could talk this out.

Five days since he'd started blaming himself, torn between believing that he'd acted like a fool and believing that he'd actually done the right thing.

But Jace was coming dangerously close to wearing out his last surviving nerve. Desperate, he pitched a lie to the boy in hopes that it would finally make Jace stop asking after Marnie.

"Because she said she had other kids to take care of. Other kids who needed her."

"But we need her," Jace insisted, clearly agitated.

"No, we don't. We're doing fine without her." No, he couldn't help thinking, they weren't. But at least he had his brothers taking turns having Jace over and watching him for a few hours. It was supposed to help him, Asher thought.

It didn't.

"Daddy, you said you never lie," Jace accused with a pout. "We're not doing fine," he told his father as if it was a fact of life. "We miss her."

More than words can say.

The thought rose in Asher's mind of its own accord. Ever since he'd listened to Marnie's voice on the voice mail and felt his heart sink, he discovered that rather than be relieved that she took the matter out of his hands, he was absolutely miserable.

Miserable because he felt he had nothing to look forward to.

Miserable because he found himself lying to his son, trying to find solace in a situation that was actually utterly intolerable to him and becoming even more so with every day that passed.

Even if he hadn't been acutely aware of the toll that not seeing Marnie had taken on him, there were his brothers, who were more than willing to point out how surly he'd become these last few days. They pointed it out on every available occasion.

They were right.

What's more, this was even worse than when Lynn had walked out on him. He hadn't thought it was possible to miss someone as much as he missed Marnie—at least, not miss someone so much and still live.

Asher felt like a lovesick fool and he found himself fighting with Jace constantly. Jace in turn had become incredibly sullen, and if Asher had thought the boy was acting out when Lynn left, it didn't even hold a candle to the way he was behaving now that Marnie had stopped coming over.

"She wouldn't do that," Jace insisted, referring to what his father had just told him. "Marnie wouldn't leave us for some other dumb kids." His small, crescent brows drew together in a thin, light brown line. "You must've made her mad," he suddenly accused. "You made her mad and that's why she went away. Just like Mommy went away because I made *her* mad."

The accusation, along with the accompanying confession, pulled Asher up short. Not because Jace was accusing him of being the reason why Marnie had gone away—when had his son become this insightful?—but because Jace thought that *he* was the reason why Lynn had left.

This was just too painfully close to the truth for Asher to allow it to stand unchallenged.

"Do you really believe that, Jace? That you're the reason why your mother left?" he asked his son incredulously. As Jace nodded, he forgot about his own pain and just focused on his son's. "We've already talked about this, Jace. I told you that you're not the reason your mom picked up and left. She just didn't want to be married to me anymore," he lied, all the while secretly worrying.

Did Jace somehow suspect that he actually *was* the reason his heartless mother had walked out?

Why?

Asher had tried so hard to place the blame elsewhere. Anywhere but on his son's small shoulders.

But this really wasn't about Lynn. At bottom, Jace wasn't talking about his mother, only Marnie. He wanted his father to do anything he could in order to get Marnie to come back again.

"Maybe if you apologize to her, you can get Marnie to come back and be with us again," Jace said hopefully, then followed up his logical projection with a heartfelt "Please, Daddy? I really, really miss her, don't you?"

Asher sighed. More than anything, he wanted to say no, that he didn't. But the truth of it was, he was getting tired of lying to both Jace *and* to himself. He missed Marnie. He missed her like hell and he didn't want to put up with the situation much longer.

"If you call her and say you're sorry, she'll forgive you. She's a nice lady," Jace was saying, still pleading his case. "She doesn't get mad all the time, like Mommy did."

"There's no guarantee that she'll come back even if I *do* call," Asher pointed out.

"But she sure won't if you don't," the boy told him simply.

Asher laughed and shook his head. The boy had obviously been born with an old mind. And, he was beginning to think, his son could argue the ears off a brass monkey. "How old did you say you were again?"

"Four." He looked up at his father, clearly confused. "You know that, Daddy."

Asher nodded. "Yes, I know that."

He also knew that Jace was right. If he didn't try to persuade Marnie to come back, she had no *reason* to come back. It was up to him to make the first move, to apologize.

God knew he'd done a lot of that with Lynn, but she'd left anyway. However, Marnie was nothing like his ex. And, in his own way, Jace had pointed that out, too. The boy's point, beneath all this, was that he wasn't being fair to Marnie, judging her by Lynn's behavior.

"You gonna do it, Daddy?" he asked eagerly, hope springing eternal in his small, young chest. "Are you gonna tell Marnie that we're sorry, that we won't ever do anything to make her go away again if she just comes back to us?" Jace asked, his eyes bright with anticipation and hope. He looked as if he was obviously moving in for the kill.

"I guess I'm going to have to. Otherwise you're not going to give me any peace, are you, big guy?" he asked with a grin.

Jace responded solemnly, shaking his head so hard his straight blond hair flew about his small face. "Uh-uh. I want her to come back to us, Daddy. And you do, too."

Definitely a gifted child, Asher thought. "Okay, Jace, you win. Let's go get you over to your uncle Wyatt's house."

Jace's face fell. Since Marnie had been gone, he had been making the rounds to his uncles' houses, going to a different one each day. He loved his uncles all right, but they were no substitute for Marnie. For one thing, their imaginations weren't nearly as much fun.

"Why?" the boy wanted to know petulantly.

"So that I can go to find Marnie and tell her that I'm—that we," he corrected himself, "are sorry."

Jace cheered as he reached up and threw his arms around his father's waist. It was obvious that the boy felt that Marnie was almost as good as back.

"Yay! I knew you would do it."

Jace had a lot of faith in his ability to persuade people. Asher could only hope that he was half as good as his son thought he was.

Chapter Sixteen

Marnie was beginning to think she was losing her mind.

There was no other explanation for the unexpected, sudden bouts of paranoia she'd been struggling with for the last couple of hours. Surrounded by horses and the group of students she was teaching, she just couldn't shake the feeling that someone, other than her students, was watching her.

Intently.

Someone, apparently, who was very good at hiding because when she looked around the perimeter of the corral and the outlining area, she didn't see anyone.

She was probably just imagining it, Marnie told herself. Maybe it was even a reaction stemming from not seeing Asher anymore.

Don't go there, don't go there, don't go there, she silently and adamantly ordered herself.

Her plan was to stay as busy as humanly possible, taking on as many students—hers and any stragglers belonging to other instructors who might have called in sick for the day—as she could in an attempt to be so busy that she didn't have a single moment to herself. Because she knew what she'd do with those moments. She'd wind up allowing her mind to stray and maybe relive a memory or two.

That was *not* the way to get over Asher Fortune. No reliving anything. No regrets. No going back. Otherwise she was going to be doomed to grieving over losing the man.

How could you lose what you never had? Marnie asked herself.

"You okay, Miss Marnie?" a little girl, Bettina Gregory, asked her, tugging on her checked shirtsleeve and looking up at her, rather concerned.

The rest of the class had been dismissed fifteen minutes ago. Bettina's mother was paying for extra time for the girl with an eye out for a spot on the Olympic equestrian team the next time around or so.

Marnie smiled down at the child, doing her best to reassure her. "I'm fine, Bettina. Just a little preoccupied," she confessed, then added an apology. "I'm sorry."

The girl didn't seem to hear the apology. She was focused on trying to understand the meaning behind her riding instructor's other words.

"Does being *preoccupied* have anything to do with that man who's been watching you today?" the girl asked innocently.

Marnie's head shot up and she was instantly alert as she scanned the immediate area again.

There *was* someone watching her.

"What man? Where?" she demanded, looking into the distance again.

She *still* didn't see anyone, Marnie thought impatiently. What was he, invisible to anyone over the age of twelve?

"Over there, by the barn," the girl said, pointing to the stables where the horses were put away for the evening.

Marnie squinted slightly, shading her eyes from the sun. She still didn't—

Yes, she did, she quickly amended.

There, in the distance, on the far side of the stables, there was the outline of a man turned in the general direction of the corral where she taught her lessons.

Asher.

"Don't worry, Bettina," Marnie said slowly, the words leaving her lips in slow motion. "He's not a stranger. I know who that is."

The little girl tilted her head as if that would make her understand what was going on better. "Then it's okay?"

That remained to be seen, Marnie thought. "Yes, it's okay."

The next moment, the little girl grinned broadly. "My mom's here!" she announced cheerfully.

Which meant that she would have no student to hide behind, Marnie realized. The little girl had been her last student of the day, and since she had stayed for some private tutoring, there was no other child in the corral for her to turn to and pretend that she was just too busy to talk to Asher.

"Don't forget to put your horse away in the stable," Marnie said automatically.

"Yes, Miss Marnie," Bettina replied obediently. Picking up the reins, she fairly skipped with her mount to the stable. "C'mon, Mom, watch me put Snowball away," she called out to her mother.

Bettina's mother looked at her watch, forced a smile to her lips and gamely made her way to the stable in her daughter's wake.

Leaving her alone and completely exposed, Marnie thought.

She had an overwhelming desire to flee, but if she did that, it would allow Asher to see that his previous behavior toward her had cut through her like a well-honed, deadly knife.

There was no way she was about to give him that sort of satisfaction.

With each step he took toward her, Asher could literally feel his courage flagging, deserting him like rats fleeing a sinking ship.

He had absolutely no idea what he was going to say to her or how he would even begin his apology.

Words had never really been a comfortable medium for him, and at a time like this, they certainly didn't come easily to his tongue. His brothers all had the gift of gab, but not him.

"Hello, Marnie," he said, his mouth feeling painfully and incredibly dry as he all but forced even these simple words out.

She barely nodded at him in response. "Asher."

He breathed a sigh of relief. "Well, at least you're not calling me names," he noted. *Or throwing anything,* he added silently. "That's a good sign."

Marnie had relived this scene over and over again in her mind as she lay awake, staring at her ceiling for the last few endless nights. On each of those occasions, all sorts of words had flowed from her tongue.

Smart words, witty words, words that knit themselves into a bulletproof shield, completely protecting her from any heartache, past or present. Words that succinctly put Asher in his place.

But right now, confronted with the actual sight of him, Marnie's mind went completely, blindingly blank.

Nothing, she thought in utter frustration. She had nothing.

"My mother never allowed those kinds of words to be said in the house," she told him in answer to his statement.

A glimmer of a smile graced his full lips. "I like your mother," he quipped.

What was *that* supposed to mean? Had he come here to taunt her? Or what?

Even just looking at him hurt, Marnie realized. "Look, I'm kind of busy here," she told him, wanting to call an end to this. She had no idea how long she could keep up this charade before she broke down and cried.

Asher looked around. "Your students are gone," he pointed out.

Her eyes narrowed. Was he challenging her now? "I do other things than teach riding."

His eyes met hers. "I know."

The way he said those two simple words caused a wave of heat to rush over her. Marnie felt herself growing angry.

"Look, this isn't going anywhere and I've got to—"

"I love you," he declared simply, without any preamble. It was all he had to offer, a simple truth that she could either accept, or trample under her feet.

He was rooting for the former.

Marnie looked at him, as dazed as if she'd just been kicked by a horse. She cocked her head like a swimmer trying to get the water out of her ears in order to hear better.

"Say what?"

"I love you," he repeated quietly.

Sincerely.

He made no move toward her, afraid that she would rebuff him if he so much as attempted to touch her. She might as well hear everything, he decided. He was past the point of being afraid of losing. Without Marnie in his life, he *was* losing.

"And I'm sorry I made such a mess of things," he told her. "I don't have a good excuse for acting the way I did. I was just… I don't know, scared, I guess," he said, finally putting a name to the emotion that had prompted him to back off initially.

"You—scared?" she echoed in disbelief.

"Yes," he told her with all due sincerity, despite the fact that it wasn't exactly something a man liked to admit. "Scared of making another mistake like I had with Jace's mother. Scared of having my heart tossed back in my face."

And his fear of that had just evaporated? She needed convincing.

"So, what are you doing here now?" she wanted to know, afraid to let herself believe that they were on the cusp of a change.

He didn't have to dig deep to give her an answer. He only had to look to his heart. "Because as scared as I am of you running over my heart, I'm even more scared of facing the rest of my life without you."

Marnie wasn't saying anything, and that made him even more uneasy. But now that he'd put it all out in front of her, he knew that there was no turning back. It was a matter of all or nothing, and he knew he couldn't bear it if the answer turned out to be the latter.

"I am willing to do anything you want," he told her. "To take it as slow as you feel comfortable with."

She looked at him for a long moment, as if weighing

his words. "What makes you think I'd feel comfortable about going slow?"

She was right, he was rushing this. They needed to go back to square one. "Okay, I can start by dating you. Then maybe, in a few months—"

Asher got no further. Marnie had placed a finger on his lips, the way she had the time that they had made love. Then it had been to stop an apology. This time it was to halt a misconception.

"No, you don't understand. I don't want to go slow. I want just the opposite," she told him, a mischievous look beginning to enter her eyes.

To say that Asher was stunned would have been one of the greatest understatements of all time.

He stared at her, trying to find his tongue. "You mean—?"

"Yup." She grinned broadly at him. When Asher made no move toward her, she teasingly prodded him. "What's the matter, are you stuck in quicksand?"

It was all the prodding he needed.

Asher cut the rest of the distance between them, wrapped his arms around her and pulled her close to his chest.

"No," he said in response to her question, just before he kissed her.

Marnie could have cried.

She was home.

"You're coming back?" Jace asked Marnie gleefully, his eyes dancing—just like the rest of him.

"I'm coming back," she confirmed. She was warm and confident in her answer. After leaving the stables, she and Asher had made what had initially been intended as a quick stop at his place before coming to pick up Jace. But quick turned out to be a relative term, and a five-minute stop turned into something just slightly under an hour.

They had a lot of lost time to make up for. But eventually, sanity prevailed and they went on to Wyatt's house, where Asher had dropped his son off before going on his do-or-die quest.

"Forever and ever?" Jace asked, all but jumping up and down now.

"For as long as you need me," she replied, doing her best to keep a straight face.

"That's forever and ever," the boy told her.

She laughed, hugging him to her. She could feel the boy's giggles vibrating against her chest. "Oh, I've missed you, Jace."

"Me, too," the boy told her. "I missed you a whole bunch. Are you gonna live here now?" he wanted to know. To him that only seemed like the logical conclusion to draw from what he was being told.

The question caught her off guard, making her stumble in her reply. She avoided looking toward Asher. "I don't think that's such a good—"

Asher slipped his arm around her shoulders as he faced his son. "Don't rush her, Jace. She's got plenty of time to move in after the wedding."

Both Jace and Marnie stared at him and cried almost in unison, "What wedding?"

"Ours," Asher answered, looking at Marnie. "That is, if you'll have me. Us," he amended as Jace tugged on his sleeve. "If you'll have us."

"So, it's a package deal?" Marnie asked, doing her best to try to keep a straight face, but, since all she felt like doing was laughing in relief, she was failing.

Had he assumed too much, gone too fast again? Asher wondered. Their pillow talk after they'd made love and just prior to heading to Wyatt's place had skimmed along the notion of marriage. He'd thought that she was on board with this, but maybe he'd gotten his signals crossed.

"Not if you don't—"

"I've always loved package deals," she told Asher as if she wasn't aware that he was trying to backtrack and possibly save face.

Jace was the first to recover. "Then it's a yes?" he asked excitedly. "You'll really marry us?"

She caressed both of their faces, a swell of affection shooting all through her. "How could I say no to two such handsome gentlemen?" she asked, looking from the son to the father.

Jace leaped up in the air, his right hand fisted and pumping in a sign of triumph. "Yay! We're getting married," he shouted happily.

The noise drew Wyatt out as Asher's brother came to see what was going on.

"What's all this damn noise all about—oh. Never

mind," he amended when he saw his brother lost in a kiss with his son's babysitter. Glancing toward his nephew, Wyatt put his hand on the boy's shoulder and ushered Jace out of the room. "C'mon, boy, your dad needs a little alone time with your sitter," he said.

"She's gonna marry my dad and be my new mom," Jace told him proudly, simply bursting with the news.

"I kinda had a feeling," Wyatt replied, glancing over his shoulder at the happy couple. The knowing grin on his face deepened. "Now let's you and me make tracks out of here, Jace."

"They want privacy, huh?" the boy asked.

Wyatt laughed, ruffling Jace's hair. "You're getting just too smart for all of us," he said in a low voice so as not to disturb his brother and the woman he assumed was going to be his sister-in-law.

Asher and Marnie never even heard them leave.

Epilogue

Marnie understood now why some people, after having something incredibly wonderful happen to them, had an almost uncontrollable desire to pinch themselves just to make sure they weren't dreaming.

That was just the way she felt.

Heaven knew she certainly felt as if she were dreaming.

But she wasn't.

She was wide awake and all this was really happening. Asher had not only told her he loved her; he'd officially proposed the very next day. Proposed and when, choking back tears, she'd said, "Yes," he had summoned their own personal little matchmaker—Jace—from the sidelines.

Grinning from ear to ear, Jace had produced the

ring box his dad had given him for safekeeping—five minutes earlier.

And then Asher had slipped the most beautiful pear-shaped, blue diamond engagement ring on her finger.

"Like it?" Jace had asked eagerly.

"Like it? I love it," she answered, almost breathless. Her eyes had shifted to Asher. "But I would have said yes even if you gave me a piece of yarn tied in a bow."

"Well, then, if that's the case, I guess I'll just take it back," Asher had teased, pretending to reach for the ring in order to take it back.

"Don't you dare!" she'd cried with a laugh, raising her left hand above her head.

And then Asher had taken her into his arms and kissed her. The kiss had been short because Jace was in the room with them, but it definitely held the promise of more things to come.

That had been a little over a week ago, and Marnie had been caught up in a nonstop whirlwind ever since.

Every day there was something else.

Gifts arriving at either his house or hers, calls from people she didn't know but were now family-to-be, wishing her happiness. There was a great deal of activity, she discovered, that was associated with becoming a member of the Fortune family.

Today, she had actually thought that the dust was finally settling a little. So she was caught completely off guard when she walked into the Red Rock country club at the invitation of Asher's cousin's new wife, Felicity, and suddenly discovered herself in the center of a bridal shower.

There were faces she knew and more faces she didn't. Much to her relief, even her mother was there. Gloria was there to lend support, and apparently from what Marnie picked up, she'd also helped with the initial planning and groundwork for this impromptu shower.

"But we haven't even set a date for the wedding yet," Marnie had protested. Asher, bless him, had offered to allow her some time to get used to the idea of becoming a wife and mother all in one swoop before they began planning the actual wedding.

"This just makes it all official, darling," her mother said, tucking her arm through hers and leading her into the center of the room. "All these lovely people just want to welcome you into the family," she assured her, then smiled. "Your 'stray' belongs to a really nice family," Gloria said with a nod of approval. And then she'd squeezed her arm. "You 'done good,' Marnie. Looks like you finally found someone who really appreciates your big heart."

Before Marnie had the chance to reply, Nicole Castleton appeared at her elbow. The smile on her lips seemed a tad forced. "Mind if I steal her for a minute, Mrs. McCafferty?"

Gloria uncoupled herself from her daughter, dropping her arm to her side. "Go right ahead, dear. My work here is done," she added with a touch of pride and just the slightest hint of a pang.

Before giving Nicole her full attention, Marnie

paused to kiss her mother's cheek. As she did so, she whispered into Gloria's ear, "You're not going to be rid of me that easily, Mom. You're stuck with me for the long run."

With a wink and a smile, she turned from her mother toward Nicole.

The latter drew her over to a corner, then turned to face her.

It was the first opportunity Marnie'd had to really focus on her friend's face. Nicole looked pale in her estimation.

Really pale.

"Nicole, are you all right?" she asked, concern entering her voice. "You look like you're coming down with something." She suppressed the desire to touch her friend's forehead to check for a fever.

Nicole responded to the latter comment with an exceedingly nervous laugh, even though there wasn't so much as a glimmer of a smile on her lips or in her wide eyes.

"I've got a really big problem, Marnie," she confided. "And I'm at the end of my rope. I don't know what to do."

Marnie forgot about the party and her own source of happiness. This was her friend, and she obviously needed help.

"What sort of a big problem?" she wanted to know so that she could do whatever it took to help Nicole in her obvious time of need.

Despite the offer and the look on Nicole's face, Marnie was in no way prepared to hear what her friend said next.

There was a second's hesitation, and then Nicole blurted out, "I need to get married, Marnie." She took a deep breath. "And fast!"

* * * * *

Don't miss the next installment in the new Special Edition continuity

THE FORTUNES OF TEXAS: SOUTHERN INVASION

Their teenage romance was thwarted by her parents. Ten years later, heiress Nicole Castleton and executive Michael Mendoza are reunited in a marriage of convenience that is intended to be strictly business—until their hearts get in the way!

Don't miss
MARRY ME, MENDOZA!
by Judy Duarte
On sale April 2013,
wherever Harlequin Books are sold.

COMING NEXT MONTH
from Harlequin® Special Edition®
AVAILABLE MARCH 19, 2013

#2251 HER HIGHNESS AND THE BODYGUARD
The Bravo Royales
Christine Rimmer

Princess Rhiannon Bravo-Calabretti has loved only one man in her life—orphan turned soldier Captain Marcus Desmarais—but he walked away knowing that she deserved more than a commoner. Years later, fate stranded them together overnight in a freak spring blizzard...and gave them an unexpected gift!

#2252 TEN YEARS LATER...
Matchmaking Mamas
Marie Ferrarella

Living in Tokyo, teaching English, Sebastian Hunter flees home to his suddenly sick mother's side just in time to attend his high school reunion. Brianna MacKenzie, his first love, looks even better than she had a decade ago...but can he win her over for the second and final time?

#2253 MARRY ME, MENDOZA
The Fortunes of Texas: Southern Invasion
Judy Duarte

Because of a stipulation in her employment contract, Nicole Castleton needs to marry before she can become the CEO of Castleton Boots. Her plan to reunite with ex-high school sweetheart Miguel Mendoza was strictly business—until their hearts got in the way!

#2254 A BABY IN THE BARGAIN
The Camdens of Colorado
Victoria Pade

After what her great-grandfather did to his family, bitter Gideon Thatcher refuses to hear a word of January Camden's apology...or get close to the beautiful brunette. Plus, she's desperate to have a baby, and Gideon does *not* see children in his future. But after spending time together, they may find they share more than just common ground....

#2255 THE DOCTOR AND MR. RIGHT
Rx for Love
Cindy Kirk

Dr. Michelle Kerns has a "no kids" rule when it comes to dating men...until she meets her hunky neighbor who has a child—a thirteen-year-old girl to be exact! Her mind says no, but maybe this one rule *is* meant to be broken!

#2256 THE TEXAN'S FUTURE BRIDE
Byrds of a Feather
Sheri WhiteFeather

Suffering from amnesia, J.D. wandered aimlessly through Buckshot Hills until Jenna Byrd offered the injured cowboy a place to stay. Slowly memories flood back to him, but what he remembers makes him want to run away from love—*fast*. Yet why can't he keep himself out of beautiful Jenna's embrace?

You can find more information on upcoming Harlequin® titles, free excerpts and more at www.HarlequinInsideRomance.com.

REQUEST YOUR FREE BOOKS!

2 FREE NOVELS PLUS 2 FREE GIFTS!

✦ HARLEQUIN®

SPECIAL EDITION

Life, Love & Family

YES! Please send me 2 FREE Harlequin® Special Edition novels and my 2 FREE gifts (gifts are worth about $10). After receiving them, if I don't wish to receive any more books, I can return the shipping statement marked "cancel." If I don't cancel, I will receive 6 brand-new novels every month and be billed just $4.49 per book in the U.S. or $5.24 per book in Canada. That's a savings of at least 14% off the cover price! It's quite a bargain! Shipping and handling is just 50¢ per book in the U.S. and 75¢ per book in Canada.* I understand that accepting the 2 free books and gifts places me under no obligation to buy anything. I can always return a shipment and cancel at any time. Even if I never buy another book, the two free books and gifts are mine to keep forever.

235/335 HDN FVTV

Name	(PLEASE PRINT)

Address	Apt. #

City	State/Prov.	Zip/Postal Code

Signature (if under 18, a parent or guardian must sign)

Mail to the **Harlequin® Reader Service:**
IN U.S.A.: P.O. Box 1867, Buffalo, NY 14240-1867
IN CANADA: P.O. Box 609, Fort Erie, Ontario L2A 5X3

Want to try two free books from another line?
Call 1-800-873-8635 or visit www.ReaderService.com.

* Terms and prices subject to change without notice. Prices do not include applicable taxes. Sales tax applicable in N.Y. Canadian residents will be charged applicable taxes. Offer not valid in Quebec. This offer is limited to one order per household. Not valid for current subscribers to Harlequin Special Edition books. All orders subject to credit approval. Credit or debit balances in a customer's account(s) may be offset by any other outstanding balance owed by or to the customer. Please allow 4 to 6 weeks for delivery. Offer available while quantities last.

Your Privacy—The Harlequin® Reader Service is committed to protecting your privacy. Our Privacy Policy is available online at www.ReaderService.com or upon request from the Harlequin Reader Service.

We make a portion of our mailing list available to reputable third parties that offer products we believe may interest you. If you prefer that we not exchange your name with third parties, or if you wish to clarify or modify your communication preferences, please visit us at www.ReaderService.com/consumerschoice or write to us at Harlequin Reader Service Preference Service, P.O. Box 9062, Buffalo, NY 14269. Include your complete name and address.

HSE13

***

How could this have happened?

Rhiannon Bravo-Calabretti, Princess of Montedoro, could
not believe it. Honestly. What were the odds?

One in ten, maybe? One in twenty? She supposed that
it could have been just the luck of the draw. After all, her
country was a small one and there were only so many rigor-
ously trained bodyguards to be assigned to the members of
the princely family.

However, when you added in the fact that Marcus Desmarais wanted nothing to do with her ever again, reasonable odds became pretty much no-way-no-how. Because he
would have said no.

So why hadn't he?

A moment later she realized she knew why: because if he
refused the assignment, his superiors might ask questions.
Suspicion and curiosity could be roused, and he wouldn't
have wanted that.

Stop.

Enough. Done. She was simply not going to think about
it—about *him*—anymore.

She needed to focus on the spare beauty of this beautiful wedding in the small town of Elk Creek, Montana. Her sister was getting married. Everyone was seated in the little church.

Still, *he* would be standing. In back somewhere by the doors, silent and unobtrusive. Just like the other security people. Her shoulders ached from the tension, from the certainty he was watching her, those eerily level, oh-so-serious, almost-green eyes staring twin holes in the back of her head.

It doesn't matter. Forget about it, about him.

It didn't matter why he'd been assigned to her. He was there to protect her, period. And it was for only this one day and the evening. Tomorrow she would fly home again. And be free of him. Forever.

She could bear anything for a single day. It had been a shock, that was all. And now she was past it.

She would simply ignore him. How hard could that be?

***

*Don't miss HER HIGHNESS AND THE BODYGUARD,
coming in April 2013 in Harlequin® Special Edition®.*

*And look for Alice's story,
HOW TO MARRY A PRINCESS, only from
Harlequin® Special Edition®, in November 2013.*

SPECIAL EDITION

Life, Love and Family

There's magic—and love—in those Texas hills!

THE TEXAN'S FUTURE BRIDE
by Sheri WhiteFeather

Suffering from amnesia, J.D. wandered aimlessly through Buckshot Hills until Jenna Byrd offered the injured cowboy a place to stay. Slowly memories seep back to him, but what he remembers makes him want to run away from love—*fast*. Yet why can't he keep himself out of beautiful Jenna's embrace?

Look for the second title in the *Byrds of a Feather* miniseries next month!

Available in April 2013 from Harlequin Special Edition wherever books are sold.

www.Harlequin.com

HSE65738